My RUNNING Club

My RUNNING *Club*

A Novel of Love, Life and Marathons

Alan Anderson

Carter Road Imprints
Houston, Texas
Carter.Road.Imprints@gmail.com

ISBN 13: 978-0-615-32765-5
ISBN 10: 0615327656

Dedicated to my wife Betsy

Contents

Memorial Park

A silent sentry stands guard over what has already been lost
Doughboys long dead, memorialized but not remembered
Replaced with links, courts, pools and running trails

Sweating business executive, meandering matron
Young mother pushing a double stroller, hard-core runner
What do they know of Argonne, Bellau Wood, Cantigny?

Six months in a muddy trench, boots soaked, clothes moldy
Food filled with maggots, dysentery my deadly mate
Then over the top, into a no man's land of flying steel

We fought so you could run, volley, tee-off and swim
Camp Logan now a park filled with life and happiness
Monument enough to the sacrifices made so long ago

Chapter 1
PROLOGUE

"That day, for no particular reason, I decided to go for a little run. So I ran to the end of the road. And when I got there, I thought maybe I'd run to the end of town. And when I got there, I thought maybe I'd just run across Greenbow County. And I figured, since I run this far, maybe I'd just run across the great state of Alabama. And that's what I did. I ran clear across Alabama. For no particular reason I just kept on going. I ran clear to the ocean. And when I got there, I figured, since I'd gone this far, I might as well turn around, just keep on going. When I got to another ocean, I figured, since I'd gone this far, I might as well just turn back, keep right on going."

—FORREST GUMP

I am not an athlete: never have been, never will be. Yet running foot races has become an important part of my life. Since college I have run twenty to thirty miles almost every week. The time spent getting ready to run, going to the park, running, coming home, and cleaning up has amounted to fifteen hours per week. This has consumed one third of my nonsleep, nonwork discretionary time. I am an addict. I feel bad when I am not running. I don't seem to ever get enough, even when I am exhausted. I impulsively sign up for marathons, momentarily forgetting how hard I will have to train and how badly I will feel at mile twenty-one. I have seriously thought about establishing a twelve-step program for runners called Runners Anonymous.

Nonrunners have a difficult time understanding why anyone would enjoy running so much that they would dedicate their life to it, especially if the person wasn't particularly good at it. What could be the possible allure of running ten kilometers in one hundred-degree heat or twenty-one miles in a cold, driving rain? I have come in from runs covered with ice and mud. When I was living in Pittsburgh, I ran outdoors every single day of the year. In Houston I once ran fifteen miles on a treadmill early Sunday morning to escape the heat and humidity outside.

For the first twenty-five years, I ran alone. Sure, I entered races, and there were other people on the roads and trails where I was running, but I didn't really run with them. I ran at the same track with the Unabomber one summer, but that didn't mean we were running buddies. My best race was a 10K in Pittsburgh where I finished in 43:30. My best marathon came in Chicago when I, unexpectedly, crossed the finish line in four hours and forty-eight minutes.

Probably my favorite race is the Rodeo Run. It is a 10K that precedes the annual parade for the opening of the Houston Livestock Show and Rodeo. Trail riders converge on downtown Houston from all over South Texas. People line the streets in anticipation of seeing several thousand horses parade by on their way to the rodeo grounds. I pretend that the crowds are out there to see us run.

My weirdest race was a 10K in Florence, Italy. It was part of the city's celebration of Saint-Jean-Baptiste Day. We started the race in darkness at nine in the evening. The race course wound its way through Florence, back and forth across the Arno River, coming to a finish in front of the Duomo. What made it weird was that the streets were not closed, the course was not marked, and it was dark.

In the early years, I ran strictly for the rush. The phrase "runner's high" suggests an altered state of mind that one is conscious of. For me the feeling was more subtle. I would lose track of place and time. Like a deep meditation, I left the world while remaining actively involved in it. It is what some pop psychologists refer to as "flow."

About a dozen years ago, I was invited to join the Memorial Park Flyers, a running club that meets twice during the week for short runs and on Saturday mornings for a long run. The group of fifteen hundred plus runners primarily consisted of people training to run marathons. The club catered to all levels of ability from walkers to local champions. I was somewhat older and heavier than the average club member. I definitely fitted into the back of the pack.

I originally had serious reservations about running with a group. I have always tended to be a loner. I enjoyed the freedom of running when and where I wanted. I am not good at small talk. I don't follow the local sports teams, recent murders, or the "affairs" of state. Most people have little idea of what I am talking about when I do try to discuss more serious matters, and I am not good at dumbing it down. I tend to be sarcastic, and many people can't take a joke. I didn't know what the club members would expect of me—besides running. I was afraid I was going to have to engage in chit-chat.

It turned out these fears were ungrounded. Most runners, or at least the ones in my club, are well educated and fairly smart. I suppose they are successful enough that they can blow massive amounts of time and energy on running. Many of them love to talk. You really didn't need to carry a radio or iPod with you. Just find a talker and you are entertained for the entire run.

The surprising thing that I discovered after running with the club for awhile was that so many of these people, even the ones that I barely knew, were willing to reveal their private lives in considerable detail. In my experience, we all build up a façade, a public persona of the person we want others to perceive. We wear particular clothes, drive a particular car, live in a particular neighborhood, and so forth to project an image. While that public image may be who we really are, in many cases, it is not. Behind that mask is another person who works hard to project an image different from who he thinks he really is. As a result, most of us have a tension in our lives between our real self and our desired self. We want to be better. We want to be more interesting. We want to please our parents. We want to please a spouse. We want to have more money. We think that humans are malleable, and with enough effort, we can be anything we want to be. After all, isn't that the great American conceit?

The reality is, of course, we can't change much, and the change that does come is seldom under our control. In spite of all our hard work and worry, things don't go the way we would like. When Jenny asked Forrest Gump, "Do you ever dream, Forrest, about who you're gonna be?" Forrest replied, "Aren't—aren't I going to be me?" That drew a laugh because Forrest naively revealed what we all know is true but hate to admit. Who has a bumper sticker saying that my kid just flunked out of State U? Who trumpets the news that he just got arrested for driving while intoxicated? No, those are things not typically talked about. There is no requirement to be truthful in advertising ourselves.

With runners, however, the inhibition on revealing our true life stories and situations seems to vanish. It starts with the fact that runners are all doing the same thing. You may be on a team, but there is no team work required. The front of the pack and the back of the pack all have to put one foot in front of the other until they reach the finish line.

The running costumes themselves are revealing. Both men and women wear rather skimpy clothes. Men don short shorts and singlets or go bare-chested. Women wear shorts or compression pants with jog bras. Most cultures have strong taboos on this kind of mixed gender activity for obvious reasons.

Then there is the smell factor. We run along sweating shoulder to shoulder, sometimes for hours. Who knows what primitive chemicals are being released? Scientists are only beginning to understand what poets and others with more practical experience have known for centuries: odors play an important role in sexual attraction.

Finally, consider the endorphins and serotonins flooding a runner's body: feel-good drugs as powerful as heroin and just as addictive. When you run in a group, the pleasant feeling that arises attaches not just to the physical activity but also to the individuals who happen to be present. Along with the visual and olfactory stimuli, these chemicals lead to an intimacy that is normally reserved for family and lifelong friends. As a result, people reveal themselves in ways they would not do if "sober."

I once saw a T-shirt that said, "Running is cheaper than therapy." In fact, running *is* therapy. An hour-long run with a dose of self-generated mood enhancers is not that much different than spending an hour on a psychiatrist's couch with a dose of Prozac. You feel better after you have told someone what your life is really like. You feel better after you have let drop the façade that you have spent so much psychic energy erecting and defending. It is positively cathartic. You feel better not just because you ran but also because you lightened your burden.

I am the Father Confessor for many of my running friends. As a management consultant, I have developed certain skills to draw information out of people. I am a good listener and know just the right questions to ask to move the story along. It is important not to reach too far and alert the subject to the level of intimacy about to be revealed. Sometimes the next question has to wait for another day. There is only so much that can be told in one session of running.

I have no way of knowing if the experiences of my friends are common to the running community in general. We talk about parents, spouses, and children; about jobs, economics, and politics; sometimes about religion; about achievements and failures; about lovers and love lost. I suspect that would be the case with most people, runners or not.

Writing about middle-aged adults means dealing with the baggage that they bring with them to any experience. Often postings on dating sites say that the person wants someone "without baggage." If you are forty-five years old and don't have baggage, I have some news for you: you died a long time ago, and they just haven't buried you yet.

Youth seek to add baggage. They are completing their educations, learning about sex, getting jobs, getting married, starting families, buying houses and furniture. All this is exciting and challenging. I have witnessed on several occasions the thrill demonstrated by a young person when they first fall in love or buy their first car or celebrate the birth of their first child. The people in my club have for the most part been there, done that, got the T-shirt.

The challenge for the middle-aged is to keep the rush coming, to find excitement in life when you have already done so many things. Even if you are in good health and are not yet focusing on the inevitable outcome of life, there is an emptiness that creeps in. You may find solace in the comfortable, ordinary things around you and in your past achievements, but it is not the same. You must now come to grips with the fact that, as the 1960s rock song observed, "Kicks just keep gettin' harder to find." Undoubtedly for many people, taking up running was an effort to keep their lives juiced.

Here are the life stories of twelve members of the Memorial Park Flyers. There are six men and six women ranging in age from late thirties to late fifties. Though I play bit parts in several stories, I have decided not to tell my own story; instead, the focus is on others. I have changed the names and details to protect the innocent and, in some cases, the guilty.

You may wonder whether this is a work of fiction or nonfiction. Is it true or not? I can't help you in that regard as I have lost my ability to discern fiction from nonfiction. Looking at the bestseller lists in the *New York Times*, it appears that what passes for nonfiction is totally made up: a fantasy produced by the writer's imagination couched in terms of verifiable facts. The stories in the following pages are true even though the specific facts are made up.

Chapter 2

KURT

My running club is called the Memorial Park Flyers. Most people just call it the Flyers. It is not really a club. It is a business venture that operates like a club but charges for joining. It was founded by Kurt Harding. Kurt was into health and fitness. He was consumed by a desire to be physically fit. Both Kurt's mom and dad were grossly obese. He often described in great detail the "globs of fat that hung from their elbows, butts, and knees. It was an effort for them just to walk from the refrigerator to the recliner."

Kurt was a fourth generation Houstonian. He descended from a long line of working-class Texans, men and women who never rose above a certain economic level, who continued to work day in and day out, who lived paycheck to paycheck. Kurt's dad was a toll taker at an underground parking lot downtown. His job involved sitting in a tiny booth for six hours a day. Each Friday afternoon, when his dad got home from work, the family would pile into their ancient Chevrolet Malibu station wagon for a trip to the Save-Big grocery outlet. Coming home from the store the car usually scraped on the driveway from the weight of the food and the people.

"I was ashamed of my family," Kurt told me. He recalled getting into a fight one afternoon with a neighbor boy who said that he couldn't play with Kurt because, "your family is white trash." Kurt never invited people to his house; he was afraid that everyone felt the same way. He was afraid to date for the same reason. Why having plenty to eat meant you were white trash was never clear to Kurt. Maybe it was other things about their house that turned people off. The yard was mostly dirt, and there was a lot of junk piled in the backyard. Their furniture was always secondhand: "It didn't make sense to my parents to buy new when the stuff at Goodwill was just as nice," Kurt said.

Kurt knew that people looked at him and thought that it was just a matter of time before he would weigh as much as his parents. But Kurt vowed to himself that he was going to be fit. He ate a healthy diet and began to work out. He used the weights at his school to build muscle mass, and he began running two or three miles a day. It was a constant struggle for Kurt to avoid his genetic fate.

When Kurt was a senior in high school, his father died of complications from diabetes, leaving Kurt responsible for his mother. When I first met him, Kurt was still living at home. He had put himself through Houston Baptist University by working in construction doing heavy labor. Not only did this provide funds for school and living expenses, but it kept him in reasonably good shape. When he graduated with a degree in kinesiology, he found a job at Southwest Fitness in member relations. He really wanted to be a personal trainer, and, after six months, the club manager let him take on a few clients.

I ran with Kurt quite a bit and one time asked him, "Have you ever seriously competed in running or any other sport, for that matter?"

I was surprised when he answered, "No. I went out for the football and basketball teams in middle school, but I didn't like the hassle of dealing with coaches. I guess I have always just competed against myself."

That competition seemed to never end. He pushed and pushed, trying to overcome his early shame and prove to himself that he was better than what other people might see. He realized that working at a health club was not the path to riches. He tried hard to expand his personal training business often working at several different clubs at the same time. He finally decided that he needed to get an advanced degree so that he could land a management job.

The University of Houston, a giant state-funded university in central Houston, offered a master's of education degree with an emphasis in sport and fitness administration. Kurt bought the school's sales pitch on the great job prospects that awaited him when he graduated. The school's marketing materials talked about jobs in "professional sports franchises, television, and university athletic programs." After he received his degree, however, he found that there were, in fact, few jobs in sports administration. For the time being, he was stuck in the personal training rat race.

His studies were not a total waste of time and money. A guest speaker at one of his classes talked about being a sports entrepreneur; that is, how to make money in sports outside of the corporate job market offered by health clubs and schools. The guy's message was, "You should just look around and see what people wanted done. You don't need to be a genius. People will tell you what they need. All you have to do is provide it."

Kurt noticed that many of his clients had gotten into running. They asked him to develop programs to train for 10k races and even marathons. Health clubs focused on building muscle or simple aerobics. To run, you needed coaches and other runners who not only ran with you, but who could support you both physically and psychologically. You needed to be outside for your long runs, not in the gym on a treadmill. At age thirty-two, Kurt had his "ah-ha" moment. The world needed someone to provide a structured running program that would take couch potatoes to the marathon finish line. He realized that he could be that person. He founded the Memorial Park Flyers in 1993.

I have to admit that I was envious of his business model. He set up the Flyers as a charity, technically it is a 501(c)(3) organization. Ostensibly, the Flyers raised money for the American Diabetes Association, and as long as he met the IRS rules, Kurt could cover his expenses including paying himself a salary. The Flyers charged people fifty bucks to meet at Memorial Park and run the streets of Houston. Kurt recruited volunteer coaches to help out by waiving the participation fee and buying them a few meals over the course of the season. As a trainee, you got a cotton T-shirt if you finished the marathon, some Gatorade to drink after your Saturday runs, and a weekly seminar from Kurt about the finer points of running.

When I joined the Flyers in 1996, it was in its fourth season. The club had gone from under one hundred runners the first year to nearly one thousand runners the year I joined. The program trained people for the Houston Marathon, which took place each January. The Houston Marathon was expanding, and the need for training was rapidly growing. In fact, the success of the Flyers had overwhelmed the available accommodations, and neighbors in the area were complaining to the city about the traffic and noise that the runners generated every Saturday morning.

The success of the Flyers was certainly the best thing that ever happened to Kurt. He had raised the annual membership fee to $70, and when enrollment hit 1,500, he was bringing in more than $100,000 a year. "I know that's not a great deal of money in the oil patch, but it's not bad pay for showing up twenty-five Saturday mornings for four hours," Kurt said. "I figure I was making about $1,000 per hour." Kurt quit his day job and focused all of his time on managing the Flyers.

Kurt also hit on the idea of sponsoring a July Fourth Race to publicize the Flyers running program. The weekend after Independence Day each year, the Flyers kicked off the marathon training season. He had heard about the July Fourth Peachtree Road Race in Atlanta. It was a 10K race that attracted fifty-five thousand runners. Houston had never had a reliable Fourth of July race. Half-hearted attempts had been made at getting one started, but they all proved to be duds. Using the Flyers, Kurt thought he could attract a good crowd, some of whom might also sign up for his training program. While not as gigantic as Peachtree in Atlanta, the 3.1-mile Flyers Firecracker 5K managed to attract over 4,000 people and became one of the largest races in Houston. At $25 per entry, the race grossed over $100,000. Here again Kurt donated a portion of the earnings to the American Diabetes Association in honor of his father.

A lot of money was coming in from the Flyers, but not everything was sweetness and light. In the first place, Kurt had a problem with women. He was almost forty, had never been married, and was still living at home with his mother. Unlike many other serially monogamous, modern, single males, he had never even had a semi-permanent girlfriend. Kurt liked to flirt with the ladies, but he did not have a clue as to how to do it. He told off-color jokes or talked about female runners in a sexually explicit way. A lot of guys might talk about the looks of a particular woman but not in front of her. Once, with many runners within earshot, he told a trainee, "Loretta, I suppose you know, you have the best boobs in the club." While Kurt's observation was probably true and while Loretta made no attempt to hide her assets, she did not appreciate the public commentary by Kurt.

The situation reached its high point, or low point depending on your perspective, when Kurt started to make out after the Saturday runs with one of the young female runners. She looked like she was just out of high school but was probably a recent college grad. However old, she was strikingly beautiful. While the rest of us were milling around drinking our free Gatorade, Kurt and the trainee could be seen at a nearby bench groping each other and kissing. Hot and sweaty in their running outfits, they made quite a scene.

Carol, one of the coaches, said to the group of women she was standing with, "That guy has no class. Why can't they go home and do that stuff?"

Sharon agreed. "It makes me sick to my stomach. I have had enough of it. He is always saying something inappropriate or touching someone. Yuck!"

"What can we do about it?" Sally wanted to know. "That's just the way Kurt is. We all know he has zero social graces. I don't think he even knows how offensive he is. Anyway he owns the club."

"I think we can do something about it. He may own the club, but we are the customers and some of us are his coaches," Sharon observed. "We can talk about it at breakfast."

At the same time that problems were growing in the Flyer organization, Kurt began running ultra-marathons. Perhaps it was his way to deal with the pressure. He would run fifty miles in Houston on Saturday and then drive to Dallas to run a marathon on Sunday. He entered various hundred-mile races, some through the desert, some over the mountains. One year he ran the Leadville Trail 100. Beginning and ending in Leadville, Colorado, it is billed as "The Race Across the Sky." The lowest point on the course is 9,200 feet, and the highest point is Hope Pass at

12,600 feet. This was particularly a challenge for someone coming from Houston where the average elevation is about sixty feet. Kurt finished in twenty-five and a half hours, earning a silver belt buckle but missing the twenty-five-hour cutoff for the gold buckle. He vowed to return the next year for the gold.

Whereas Kurt could have used his newfound wealth to buy a BMW or a house, he preferred to spend it on his ultra races. He had to hire a support team and transport them to distant events. Like the men that hang around pro football and basketball players, these guys depended on Kurt for favors. He paid them for helping with the club, for working at the Flyers Firecracker 5K, and for providing support on his various athletic adventures. His "boys" didn't like anyone criticizing Kurt. One of them told Sharon, "If you don't like the way Kurt runs the Flyers, get out. It's a free country. Nobody is forcing you to come. Anyway, you don't understand that this is an athletic club not the Girl Scouts."

The unrest in the club wasn't only about Kurt's behavior or management style. It had become clear to a lot of people that a marathon training program like the Flyers offered a bigger opportunity than Kurt had ever imagined. Marathons were becoming increasingly popular among baby boomers. Some of the Flyers coaches made plans to establish similar programs around Houston. Others, not associated with the Flyers, were also getting into the business. Jeff Galloway, an Olympic runner and one-time holder of the American ten-mile road race record, established a national marathon training organization. Like any successful business, the Flyers organization was facing some serious competition, but Kurt didn't really want to be a businessman, notwithstanding his advanced degree in sports administration.

Dissatisfaction among the women in the Flyers was a serious business issue. The biggest growth in the popularity of marathon running was among women. Races were extending the finishing times to accommodate slower runners, many of which were female. Kurt's inability to relate to women was alienating an important part of his customer base. Some were starting to migrate to other training programs.

Kurt came to me one Saturday after a run and told me that he needed some help. He hadn't kept the books very well, and the IRS was questioning some of his expenses. Also the administrative burden of dealing with sponsors, insurance companies, T-shirt vendors, and so forth was overwhelming him. Many entrepreneurial types get tired of their ventures once they are successful, and the operation turns from being an exciting adventure to being a lot of drudge work. Kurt asked me to go to work for him and manage the business side of the Flyers.

His request was flattering but naïve. My salary at that time was more than the entire annual revenue of the Flyers. I had no interest in becoming Kurt's business manager, though I told him that he did indeed need to find someone to help him manage the Flyers. Kurt ended up choosing Bill Smithers, one of the most obnoxious of his male sycophants, as the vice president of operations and head coach.

Many people were not pleased with Kurt's choice. Most of the participants in the Flyers thought it was a club, like the Rotary or PTO. Many of them had been members of other running clubs in Houston and elsewhere. In those clubs there were by-laws, and the club officers were elected. They expected a treasurer's report at quarterly or annual meetings so that everyone could see where the club money was being spent. They couldn't understand how Kurt managed to call all the shots without consulting anyone else.

In Kurt's mind, the entire Flyers operation was a business that he owned. As the owner, he could do whatever he wanted with it. He realized that he had to be concerned about his customer base, but he didn't appear to understand that the assistant coaches had considerable clout as they were the ones who interacted directly with the client runners.

The appointment of Bill as head coach was the catalyst that led to a revolt among the rank and file members. Sharon, Sally, and Carol seemed to be the most upset and the most ready to take action. Though each had been a member of the Flyers for several years, Sharon was clearly the ring leader. She didn't have a regular nine-to-five job, but she had plenty of money. The three dissidents and their supporters liked to emphasize the social aspect of training and racing over the physical aspect. The runs, for them, were more like coffee klatches on the move with Gatorade. They wanted the Flyers to be a social club run by the members. Sharon sent out an e-mail to all the Flyers that she knew informing them of the selection of Bill as head coach and calling a meeting at her house the next Sunday evening.

At Sharon's meeting, she circulated a petition asking that by-laws be established for the Flyers and that an accounting of funds be made to the members. It also called for an election to select officers. The petition was to be presented at the coaches' training session scheduled for that Wednesday evening. The plan was to present the petition to Kurt and then stage a walkout. Sharon was convinced that she could bring enough pressure to get her way.

I tried to stay on the sidelines. I could see the agitators' points, but why not just start another club if they didn't like the way Kurt was running the Flyers? It soon became clear to me that the issue was money. Anyone could do the math and see that the "club" was pulling in close to two hundred grand a year and there was the possibility of expansion. A chance to get a cut of the action does funny things to people. Everyone recognized that Kurt had done all the hard work to get the Flyers going, but he was vulnerable in several areas and Sharon was prepared to go after him "no holds barred."

By Wednesday night, the petition had over three hundred signatures from both male and female runners, all of whom were coaches or past participants in the Flyers program. Several of the runners who signed the petition were lawyers. They felt that Kurt was probably not following the letter of the law in his operation of the Flyers. They needed more information before saying for sure, but things didn't look right to them.

The training session was held in a large room at the golf center in Memorial Park. That night it was standing room only. Kurt started the meeting with his usual welcoming statement. "I want to welcome everyone back for another fantastic Flyers season. I don't need to tell you that this program could not exist without your support and enthusiasm. We have enjoyed tremendous growth, and it has gotten to the point where I need to spend more of my time on administrative matters. Toward that end, I have decided to appoint a head coach to manage the marathon training program this year. Bill, come on up here."

As Bill made his way to the front, there was a rustle of anticipation in the room. With Bill standing beside him, Kurt continued, "I think most of you know Bill Smithers. Bill has been with the Flyers since the beginning and has already been handling much of the logistics for me. From now on, he will be the Flyers head coach and the person in charge of our training programs. Bill, you can take it from here."

Before Bill could say a word, Sharon stood up and interrupted the proceedings. Sharon, a self-confident person, did not hesitate to immediately explain to Kurt what she had in mind for the club. "I'm sorry to interrupt, Kurt, but we're not going to go along with this. I know you own the Flyers but, if you don't change the way things are run around here, you're going to lose most of your coaches and a lot of your runners." At that point there were some boos and some clapping in the room as folks began to choose up sides. Sharon let the noise die down before continuing, "I have a petition here with hundreds of signatures asking that by-laws be established for our club. This club is important to me. As you can see, it is important to many of us. We aren't going to abandon it without a fight."

Kurt had evidently heard what was coming and was not surprised by the petition or by Sharon's speech. In fact, he had prepared his own speech. "The Flyers is not a club; it's a business, my business," he told Sharon, "and I'll run it as I see fit. If you or anyone else tries to undermine my operation, I will take the necessary legal steps to stop you." He was not conciliatory in the slightest. At that point, most of Sharon's supporters headed for the exit. Kurt's buddies were hooting at them as they left, shouting, "Take your tea party elsewhere!" and "This is a running club, not the Junior League!"

Carol, another of the ring leaders in the rebellion, now took the floor. Carol was a lawyer and a CPA. In a calm, no-nonsense tone, she told Kurt that he had three problems: "First, you've engaged in repeated sexual harassment of female runners in the club. Offensive comments. Lovemaking at workouts. These are not the actions of a sensible businessperson. Several women are preparing to press charges against you and the Flyers. Secondly, many of us suspect you are violating the IRS rules regarding charitable organizations. Because you have represented to us that we are members of a club, we plan to file a lawsuit to obtain the financial records of the Flyers back to its date of origination. Finally, we're tired of your cadre of friends who, like you, are insensitive and rude to the rest of the membership. This is not your own personal fiefdom where you and your insiders can run roughshod over everyone else."

Kurt was clearly shaken. He had the look of a person who had just been in a bad car wreck and could see his smashed arm dangling from his shoulder. He knew his life had suddenly changed for the worse, but he couldn't quite tell why it happened and where things would go. It was a look of disbelief.

The people up against him were the same people who had always put him down when he was growing up: the wealthy, educated elite that got their way at the expense of the little guy. He had made a success of the Flyers, but could he take on a group that had free access to first-class lawyers and accountants? They probably also had political contacts at city hall that could make trouble for him over using a city park and the city streets for business purposes.

"Carol, you better be careful what you say. You may not like the way I run the club, but this is my business. If you don't like it, get out. You keep accusing me of breaking the law or harassing my runners and you're going to hear from my lawyer. I'm not going to take that from you or anybody else."

I had planned to stay quiet but didn't. "Look, a large meeting is no place to hash out these issues. Let's get a smaller group together. We could even do it this week."

Kurt's confidence had been rattled by the harassment charges and by the size of the walkout. Pointing his finger at Sharon, he said in a loud voice, "I'm willing to meet, but you are not going to steal my business from me."

Carol, who realized that she had gone too far in a public meeting, responded, "No one is trying to steal anything here. If you would sit down and listen to what we have to say, maybe we can work this out."

I sensed a willingness on both sides to talk. "Okay then. We can meet at my office on Friday. All of you need to think about what you want to accomplish and what would be in the best interest of the Flyers."

Chapter 3
LORETTA

"Get your things together, Loretta. We have to go," Loretta's mother said.

Loretta looked out the window. It was still dark. A cool wind rustled through the tree by her window. Loretta started to cry. "I don't want to go. I like my class. Can't we just stay until the end of school?" She knew there was no use arguing. She had heard her parents talking—her dad had been fired again; money would be short. Outside the pickup truck was loaded with the furniture, and the rest of their stuff was packed in the car. Loretta found a place in the backseat and crawled in.

Loretta was eight years old, and her family had moved four times in the last two years. Sometimes they had an apartment and sometimes a mobile home. They had been living for the last few months in a two-bedroom duplex. She wondered where they were headed now.

Loretta's father was the Reverend James Hargrove. He was the pastor of a flock at the Church of the First Nazarene in Mansfield, a farming town southwest of Dallas. The Church of the First Nazarene was an independent, Pentecostal church that followed a strict literal reading of the King James Bible. In addition to his sermons, the Reverend Hargrove spoke in tongues and practiced faith healing once a week on Thursdays. He was a tall man with large hands and spoke in a deep, southern drawl. For many of the children in his church, and adults too for that matter, he was the embodiment of God.

Tending to a small, poor congregation never paid enough to support a family, so James worked as a clerk in local paint and hardware stores. He knew a lot about home construction and tools. He never had a hard time getting hired on, but before long, he usually had problems with the boss.

James had a specific idea of how the world should operate, much of which he had learned from his frequent chats with God. This knowledge primarily had to do with the proper behavior for a Christian. For instance, drinking alcohol or coffee was not allowed in the Hargrove house, and, of course, no cigarettes or other drugs were tolerated. James told everyone that his only vice was an occasional glass of iced tea.

Reverend Hargrove objected to the traditional celebrations that occurred around important biblical events. He had closely studied the development of the early church and knew that both Easter and Christmas were pagan holidays the Roman Church had adopted to sell the Lord's message to the heathens. Santa Claus and the Easter Bunny were not recognized as legitimate Christian figures by the Hargroves, and Loretta was required to go to the principal's office whenever parties were held at her school for those holidays.

James also had particularly strong ideas about how business should be conducted. For instance, one boss insisted that James "upsell," encouraging customers to consider premium paints even though the boss knew all the paints were basically the same quality. Also, many so-called "sales" were bogus and involved claiming that items had been discounted when actually they were marked at their normal price. People didn't buy paint often enough to realize they were being fooled. James frequently talked about turning his bosses into the Better Business Bureau or even reporting these practices to the consumer advocate on Channel 4. But before he could get around to it, he would pick a fight over some minor issue and get himself fired.

Then a miracle happened. Loretta's mother, Sarah, was promoted to manager at the cleaning company she worked for in Arlington, a rapidly growing town just north of Mansfield and halfway between Dallas and Ft. Worth. Sarah actually worked for a disaster recovery firm, but James always called it a cleaning company. He felt that a proper Christian husband should be the sole provider for his family and was embarrassed by the fact that Sarah had a responsible job. When Sarah began making more money than James and could support the family on her own, James decided that this was a sign from above directing him to focus on his ministry. He quit his job at the Sherwin-Williams paint store where he had been working for the last few months.

Everything now seemed to be going pretty well for the Hargroves. At least there were no more worries about money. They weren't rich, but there was plenty to eat and they soon moved to a nice house in north Arlington near the Texas Rangers baseball stadium. Loretta liked her school and did better in her classes, since she had been able to stay in one place for the entire school year.

Her only problem was that, with her mother busy rescuing people from physical disasters and her father busy rescuing people from spiritual disasters, Loretta was left to take care of the house and her brothers. She had to cook the meals, vacuum the floors, wash the dishes, and do the laundry. She rose every morning to cook breakfast and pack sack lunches for the boys. After school she cleaned the house and prepared supper. When she was old enough, she even did the grocery shopping.

As a result of all her responsibilities, Loretta developed the habit of not getting much sleep. She knew that her mother expected all the chores to be done when she got home, so she always cleaned the house and did the dishes before starting her homework. Once, Loretta forgot to pick up some toys that the boys had been playing with after dinner. Loretta's mom didn't get home until after midnight and was in a bad mood. As she crossed the darkened living room, Sarah tripped and fell. Loretta was still up working on an English report due the next day. When she heard a crash followed by a loud curse, Loretta knew trouble was coming.

Sarah stomped into Loretta's bedroom and yelled, "Is it too much to ask you to help out around the house? Here I am working till after midnight so you can have everything in the world a girl could possibly want and what do I find? A house so messy that I trip and about break my neck."

Loretta tried to explain, "Those are the boys' toys. They must have gotten them out after I already picked up. I'm sorry. I didn't mean it."

"Don't sass me, young lady. I don't care whose toys they are. You are the one who is supposed to pick 'em up. Now bend over."

Her mom pulled Loretta's pajama bottoms down and gave her bare butt a good spanking with the belt she had been wearing. Loretta had learned to hold back her tears until her mother left the room. Tonight she still had a paper to finish.

Such episodes only reinforced Loretta's determination to leave home as soon as she finished high school. Loretta loved science and wanted to learn more about it. She was thinking about doing research, and her chemistry teacher had recommended her for a small scholarship. When it came through, she had enough money to pay for the tuition at the University of Texas at Arlington in, what was now, her hometown.

When her father heard about Loretta's decision to go to the nearby campus of UT, he was very pleased. "Loretta, you got a good deal on that scholarship and since school is so close you can just stay here. I know your mother still needs help around the house."

Staying at home was not part of Loretta's plan. "Dad, I'm going to live over at the dorm. I think it will be more fun."

"That's exactly what I'm worried about. There are a lot of bad influences out there, evil influences. You are a pretty, young girl. You know enough to know what boys want to do to you."

Blushing, Loretta assured her father, "I'm not into that kind of stuff. I want to study. I want to be a chemist."

"If you go over there, you are on your own. Money is tight. I suppose I can get one of the ladies from the church to come over and clean the house. That'll cost me something."

"I just want to try it. I can get a job. If it doesn't work out, I'll come home." Loretta moved to the dorm in September and never lived at home again.

The scholarship paid for tuition, but Loretta had to come up with money for fees, books, and living expenses. She waited tables, sold clothes in a boutique, and tutored to make ends meet. In the summer she worked at *Six Flags Over Texas*, a large theme park in Arlington. She started out cleaning tables at the Mexican restaurant there and eventually worked her way up to food service manager.

Her undergraduate years were nothing but work and studying. There was not much time for the college party scene. Loretta's hard work paid off though, and she won a scholarship to go to graduate school at the University of Texas in Austin where she planned to pursue a PhD in chemistry. The chemistry department even offered her a job as a lab assistant, and, for the first time in her life, it looked like Loretta had things under control.

Austin was a happening place. It was the center of Texas music and the hippie scene. It was all exciting to Loretta who began to hang out on Sixth Street where the hippies congregated. Several clubs and bars catered to the students and to the cloud of nonstudents that had descended on Austin. For the first time in her life, Loretta yearned to be a social creature; someone who went out on dates, who wore makeup and tried new hair styles; someone the boys paid attention to.

As a budding academic, Loretta looked to books for advice. She found *Sex and the Single Girl* by Helen Gurley Brown. It, and Brown's magazine, *Cosmopolitan*, provided just the guidance Loretta needed. She began wearing sexy outfits. Loretta had a Rubenesque body and was not afraid to let the guys see what she had. Once she got their attention, she complimented them on anything and everything she could think of. She was shameless with the compliments. She discovered men really believed the good things she said about them. Finally, she pretended to like sex. She talked about giving blow jobs or her favorite positions. What red-blooded Texas male wouldn't like talking dirty to a cute girl with no bra under a thin dress who told him he was cool?

At the beginning of her second year at Texas, Loretta met Chuck Cambell. He had "CC" tattooed on his arm over two lightning bolts. He was blond, muscular, and rode a Harley. He seemed to have plenty of money and was just drifting around Austin being part of the scene. He could play a guitar and sometimes sat in with local bands. He was quiet but also a hell raiser. Chuck liked Loretta. He especially liked it when she danced up front with the band while he was playing. After one wild evening and a few too many beers, Chuck asked point blank, "Loretta, I don't get it. You're all the time talking about screwing, but you won't do it with me. Don't you like me?"

"Chuck, we make out just about every night. I don't complain much when you put your hand down there or pull my top up. In fact, I like it. Don't you?"

"Sure, I like feeling you up, but that ain't screwing."

The truth was that Loretta was a virgin. She followed the Bible and believed you shouldn't fornicate before you were married. What would Jesus think of her if she got pregnant? What would the Reverend Hargrove think? She knew she could never get an abortion. So she told Chuck, "I am not on the pill and I am really afraid of getting pregnant. You know I love you, but I want to wait till I'm married to have sex."

"Are you trying to tell me you are not going to do it unless I marry you? Well, I ain't waiting. You were at the club. It's full of horny coeds. I need some relief here," he said pointing to his protruding crotch.

Loretta decided then and there that blow jobs were okay. She couldn't find anything in the Bible that said blow jobs were wrong, and at that time Austinite Kinky Friedman had a popular song that went, "Eatin' ain't cheatin'. It's no disgrace." She didn't like it, but she did it. Chuck seemed satisfied for the moment.

Chuck invited Loretta to go to New York that Christmas to meet his family. He was thinking about making this a long-term relationship and wanted to see what his father thought of Loretta. He expected that there might be a cultural clash. Chuck's dad, Fred Cambell, was wealthy. He owned three auto parts stores: one on Long Island and two in North Jersey. The Cambell compound on Long Island included a main house and three smaller houses, one for Chuck's sister, one for his brother, and one for Chuck. His brother and brother-in-law both worked in the family business. Everyone expected that after sowing his wild oats, Chuck would move home and go to work for his dad, as well.

Loretta didn't know what to make of Chuck's family and the way they lived. It was quite a contrast to the way she had grown up. People dressed for dinner and had cocktails by the fireplace at six every evening. They ate funny smelling cheeses and toast that had some kind of liver on it. And, Chuck's family was definitely into drinking. The first evening she was there, Fred asked, "Loretta, what can I fix you to drink?"

"Thanks, I think I will just have a beer."

"No, I meant a real drink. How about a Margarita? Isn't that the national drink of Texas?" Fred was an expert at mixing strong drinks in glasses that were deceptively large. He wondered what Loretta was like after she got tipsy.

Loretta looked around the room. Several people were drinking wine. "Well, then I guess I will just have some pink wine, if you have any."

With his back turned to Loretta, Fred poured some Merlot and some Chardonnay into a glass. He handed it to her with a smile thinking, "Now I know all I need to know about this girl."

On Christmas Eve Chuck's family all got potted, and the internal family tensions that were normally hidden emerged in full force. People were yelling at each other, and there were some tears. Loretta felt very out of place. The excessive drinking on the night of the Lord's birthday and all this carrying on about who did what to whom seemed more suitable for high school students than for sophisticated, adult New Yorkers. Fred noticed that Loretta was not joining in, and when he got a chance, he sat down beside her and asked, "This is a pretty weird family, don't you think?"

Loretta politely ducked the question and said, "Mr. Cambell, this is just not the way we celebrate Christmas back home."

Chuck's dad nodded as if commiserating with her then sighed, leaned back, and took a sip from his glass. "Loretta, I am sure you are a nice girl, but you wouldn't be comfortable living here. We are just too different. Chuck needs a woman that understands his family and can fit in with our lifestyle, even though we are a strange tribe. You just aren't that girl."

"Isn't that for Chuck to decide?" Loretta asked.

"Not really. Chuck is into fun right now, and I am sure you are a lot of fun," he said. After pausing for a moment and giving Loretta's bust line a lecherous look, he continued, "Eventually, Chuck will want to settle down and come home to work for me. Let me put it this way: there are a lot of girls that can offer him sex, but only one father that can offer him money. I know my son better than you do, and he will take the money."

Loretta went from being polite to being angry. She rose from the sofa and said, "We'll see about that."

23

Fred seemed amused by her. As she walked away, he said just loudly enough for her to hear, "Yes, we will." His quiet assurance frightened Loretta more than his words.

Loretta thought she could eventually charm Chuck's family into accepting her, but she needed to get a proposal out of him first. It was obvious that Chuck was worried about what his dad would do if they got married. More than likely his father had explained Chuck's options to him and told him exactly what he thought about Loretta.

Back in Austin for New Year's Eve, Chuck and Loretta partied with their old gang down on Sixth Street. When the police finally shut the party down, Loretta invited Chuck to spend the rest of the night at her place. They went all the way. It was against the Bible and Jesus, but it worked. Chuck forgot all about his dad. He moved in with Loretta. It was a done deal. By April she was pregnant, and Chuck proposed.

It is surprising how fast people's lives can change for the worse. Good changes often develop over months or years. Bad changes can happen in minutes. Loretta assumed that Chuck would get a job and that she would finish her PhD. She had a good chance of joining the faculty at one of the smaller Texas colleges after she graduated. Chuck assumed his parents would accept Loretta once they were married and had produced a grandbaby. He had not thought about getting a job. He wasn't sure what he could do.

Chuck's father immediately cut off his allowance. No one from Chuck's family attended their wedding, which was held at Reverend Hargrove's church in Mansfield. They didn't offer an excuse; they just didn't come. Chuck told Loretta he had no idea of how he would be able to support the two of them and a baby without his allowance. He agreed to sell his Harley, but that wasn't the same as a steady income. In May, Loretta got her master's degree in chemistry but about the only job she was qualified for was analyzing urine and blood samples at a medical lab.

The newlyweds each took aptitude tests to see what jobs fit their skills and interests. Loretta scored high on sales aptitude, something she must have inherited from her dad. The test indicated Chuck would do well in an outdoor job where he could work with his hands. Compaq Computer in Houston was looking for salespeople with technical backgrounds. Loretta liked the idea of living in Houston. It had been good to be away from her mom and dad during graduate school, and she didn't want to go back to Dallas.

She applied for the Compaq job and took the offer when it came. The couple found an apartment in Tomball, a northwest suburb of Houston near Compaq's corporate offices. After they relocated, Chuck began working in construction. Their son was born on Christmas Day.

Loretta started running in 1998, twelve years after she left Austin. People run for many different reasons. Loretta was running to get out of the house, to get away from Chuck, and to get back some of her self-esteem. She had not married a very helpful or reliable husband. Maybe it should have been obvious to her what kind of man Chuck was, but she loved him and love does, occasionally, blind us all. Loretta took care of the house and the kids and had a full-time job. Chuck bragged that he never changed a dirty diaper. He also liked to stop by an ice-house on the way home from work for a few beers, sometimes not getting home till after midnight.

His construction jobs paid well enough when he could find work, but the boom and bust cycles in the Houston economy meant that he was often unemployed. He did manage to save enough to buy another Harley, and he joined the Katy Kruisers Klub, a motorcycle club in the nearby town of Katy. The club's jackets had a Confederate flag on the back with KKK, the first letters in their name, prominently featured.

Each weekend the Kruisers went on a club ride, often taking overnight trips to campgrounds in the Houston vicinity. Most of the guys were single and brought their girlfriends on the outings. A few of the married guys brought their wives, but most either came by themselves or brought a girlfriend along. On Saturday nights, the camp agenda consisted of sitting around a campfire drinking booze and smoking dope. Loretta made it clear to Chuck that she had no interest in his biker friends.

During the summer of 2002, many of the Memorial Park Flyers were training to run the Chicago marathon in October. I had run it several times, and it was one of my favorite races. As part of our training for Chicago, we did a fifteen-mile run in mid-August. The heat and humidity was always stifling, but if you were going to run a fall marathon, you have to do it, like it or not.

The Saturday morning of our fifteen-miler, I saw Loretta throwing up in the bushes before we started. I could tell that she had been crying. When she had somewhat regained her composure, I walked over to her and asked, "Loretta, what's wrong?"

"Oh, I'm just not feeling well this morning. Didn't get much sleep last night."

"Maybe you should skip the run. I can wait and run with you tomorrow morning, if you like."

"No, I have to teach Sunday school," she said. "I can make it today."

"Okay, but I'm going to pace you. You have a bad habit of going out too fast on these long runs."

Almost immediately after we started running, Loretta blurted out, "He told me it was no big deal. He said they were all friends just like the Flyers. Right! I wonder how long this has been going on."

"Wait a minute. Wait a minute. What are we talking about here?" I asked.

"It's a woman that rides with Chuck. She has her own bike and goes on most of the Kruiser weekend trips. Anyway, last Thursday she calls just after dinner and says she has to see him. I asked if it couldn't wait until the weekend, but Chuck said no. He was gone all night. When he got back, he looked totally washed out. He told me that there were big problems. The woman's husband, who had to work last weekend and couldn't ride with the Kruisers, was filing for divorce, and he wanted sole custody of their three kids. Chuck told me that this guy thought that his wife had had three-way sex with him and another Kruiser during the trip last weekend. The wife is denying it, and now Chuck might be subpoenaed to testify at the divorce trial."

"Was it true?" I asked.

"That's what I asked Chuck. He hemmed and hawed around a bit before admitting that the three of them did all get into the same tent. It started off as a joke. You know: 'The mosquitoes are pretty bad out here. Maybe we better get in the tent.' The next thing Chuck knew, this other guy and the woman were inside her tent making a bunch of noise.

When he went in to see what was going on, he found them both with their clothes off rolling around naked on a queen-sized air mattress. She grabbed Chuck's crotch and started playing with it. He says he just made a mistake.

"I asked him how many times he had made that mistake before. He couldn't remember for sure. This crowd tends to get out of hand sometimes. Then I asked if all she did last Saturday was play with him? He said he thought so. He couldn't really remember. Sometimes the three of them would just be in a pile and it wasn't clear who was doing what to whom. The more he talked, the more he seemed to enjoy rubbing my face in it. Maybe he and the guy were screwing each other. I would believe anything now. The bottom line is that the woman's husband didn't like her doing other guys when he wasn't around."

"Will Chuck leave you for this woman if she really gets a divorce?" I asked.

"No way. She's a cashier at a Cabana Carwash. She can't support him like I do. Anyway, what I am really worried about is that this will get into the papers if the divorce goes to court. If it does, all of the neighbors will know and my kids will find out what a lowlife their father is."

I assured her, "This is not likely to go to court. The husband is just mad because he wasn't there to join in the fun. It sounds like messing around with multiple partners is not unfamiliar territory with this group. Once the husband cools down I bet that they will patch things up." As it turned out, that is what happened.

Loretta didn't want a divorce either. I don't know if she still loved Chuck. She talked about her kids an awful lot, and she was still a devout Christian. At some level maybe she felt Chuck could turn things around, maybe he could be saved. What she needed at the moment, however, was someone to authenticate her as a woman. Was there a man who would pay attention to her as a person and not think of her as merely a meal ticket and a maid? She had obviously been living a nightmare, and this incident was a crushing psychological blow.

To bolster her self-esteem, she dusted off the old *Cosmo* techniques she had used in Austin to attract men and went on the hunt among the Flyers. I guess because I was nearby and had been a sympathetic ear, she went after me first. This time she started with the compliments. "There is my hero!" "You are really running strong!" "Have you lost some weight?" "You are really looking good."

Next, came the skin. After a run, she would put on a loose fitting top and then make sure to bend over just enough so I could see down her shirt. Sometimes I would be talking to her, and she would stick a thumb in each side of her running shorts pulling them out far enough to expose her white bikini briefs which usually had a heart or rose embroidered on them. She would look down so that her eyes led mine to the show. One time, after a run, I saw her with a towel around her shoulders. I said, "Show me something, mama." It was a standard line of mine when I saw one of the girls changing. Damned if she didn't throw the towel back and reveal her naked body. I was surprised and impressed.

Loretta began running with me every Saturday and hanging around with me after the runs. She usually had some dirty joke to tell or a funny comment to make about one of the other runners, male or female. Sometimes she would tell me in great detail about a recent love session she had had with Chuck. I was flattered by Loretta's obvious interest in me.

When we finally went to Chicago for the marathon, Loretta made sure we were together all the time. We sat next to each other at the group dinners and walked around the city together window shopping. On the plane back to Houston, she began talking about running other out-of-town races together and going for a drink after our training runs. Finally, I told her, "Loretta, I'm married."

"I know that, silly. I met your wife at the pasta party before the Houston Marathon last January."

"She doesn't let me date anymore. I can't go out with you."

Loretta was quiet for the rest of the trip home. I don't think that she recognized that she was talking about dating. And maybe she wasn't. Maybe it was just a generational difference in our perspectives. At fifty-seven, I was almost old enough to be her father.

After Chicago, Loretta was still friendly but didn't hang around me much. She began to sit next to other guys at breakfast, some married, some not. Then she started missing a lot of the Flyers training runs.

When I bumped into her at an Astros baseball game, she told me she was running up in Tomball with a fellow from her office. Every now and then, Loretta would show up for a Saturday run. On those occasions, she talked mostly with the women runners.

Chapter 4
MYLES

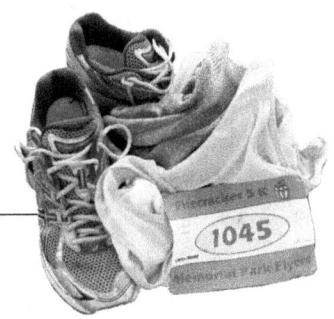

Parents abuse their children in different ways. The dysfunctional family was the hot topic among self-help gurus until somebody pointed out that all families are dysfunctional, especially when it comes to the relationship between parents and children. Early TV shows depicted the life of what was then considered to be the perfect family: a working father, a homemaking mother, and polite, well-behaved children. That certainly is not the reality today—and wasn't even back then. Parents either do their own thing, neglecting their children, or they focus on parenting to the point of stifling their children's freedom and development. Occasionally, a happy medium exists. This was not the case with the Tucker family.

Hub Tucker went overboard when it came to parenting. He had risen above his own poor, dirt farmer start to become a successful engineer, and he planned to pass the Tucker family baton to his son Myles to continue the forward progress. Upward and onward! From an early age, Myles had heard the lecture about how hard his father's life had been and how through hard work and sacrifice his father had gotten ahead. It was now Myles's turn to take the next step for the family.

Hub felt that the Grapevine, Texas, public school curriculum was sadly lacking in the sciences and mathematics, and he was probably right about that. The few thousand people who lived in Grapevine cared more about whether the football team made it to the bi-district playoff game held each year at the Cowboy's stadium in Irving, than about how the seniors did on their college placement exams. So, beginning when he was in third grade, Myles was home schooled in the evening. Hub mounted a blackboard in the living room and, after dinner, taught his son algebra, chemistry, and physics.

Theoretical concepts were put to practical use in the design and construction of a Soap Box Derby car. The Soap Box Derby is a competition in which young contestants design and build, on their own, a car to race down a hill, powered only by gravity. As a kid, Hub had wanted to enter the Soap Box Derby but never got the chance. Now he wanted Myles to fulfill his dream. Detailed blueprints were prepared, and each part was handcrafted out of wood. While, as required by the contest rules, Myles did all the work, he was closely supervised by his dad. Some days he was in the shop for over twelve hours. When he complained, he heard the old lecture about getting ahead.

Hub was also a big fan of the Boy Scouts. In fact, he was Cub Master for Myles's pack and Scout Master for Myles's troop. Myles didn't really enjoy camping. He had several disasters on campouts, including one incident in which a close friend was killed. But camping wasn't the point. Hub wanted Myles to earn the rank of Eagle. He had only made First Class, and this was another opportunity for Myles to move the family forward.

The Eagle required earning twenty-one Merit Badges. Scouts shared information on which badges were the easiest to earn and which took real work. Myles quickly figured out the shortest and easiest path to Eagle. His father was beaming at the award ceremony when, as Scout Master, he presented the Eagle to his son. In retrospect, Myles realized that the Boy Scouts had taught him how to cut corners and game the system to get ahead. Skills that proved to be of considerable value later in life.

Of course, Hub thought that young people needed to understand that making money was a fundamental part of life. He often told Myles, "No one is going to give you a living, son, you have to work for it." Myles mowed lawns during the summer and worked part-time at the local Penney's store during the holiday season. In the ninth grade, he became a carrier for the *Dallas Morning News*. He was up at 4:00 a.m.

every morning to deliver papers. Before he got his driver's license, this meant a five-mile bicycle ride around his route, often in the cold and dark and, a few times, even in the snow. He would return home with just enough time to clean up for school and grab a bite to eat. Myles's mother once told him how proud she was that her son was a paperboy. A neighbor thought the regimen forced on Myles was severe enough to qualify for child abuse and reported the family to the authorities. Nothing ever came of it.

Even with all of these extracurricular activities, Myles shined at school. He took the hardest classes his school offered and made straight A's. He was president of the Science Club and Math Club. When the physics teacher got sick, he taught the class for two weeks. He was a National Merit Scholar and made a perfect score on the Math College Entrance Exam. He was valedictorian and gave a speech at his graduation ceremony. The local newspaper even published an article about him under the headline, "Boy Genius Attends Conference."

Myles was all set to follow in his father's footsteps and attend Rensselaer Polytechnic Institute in Troy, New York. He wanted to be a space scientist, and RPI had one of the premier programs in that field. He also wanted to escape his family, and New York seemed far enough away that he would not be expected to come home often. Unfortunately, when he visited the campus in February, a blizzard dropped a foot of snow on Troy. Once the snow stopped, the wind-chill factor fell to near zero. New York weather was quite different than the weather Myles was accustomed to in Texas, and people in New York were different, too. They talked differently and dressed differently than Myles's friends. He didn't like them or their snow.

Although he had made up his mind on that trip that he didn't want to go to RPI, it took Myles six weeks to muster the courage to tell his dad. By that time, it was already April of his senior year, way too late to be applying to other elite colleges. His physics teacher, nonetheless, suggested that he contact Rice University. Myles didn't know much about Rice except that it had a football team and was in Houston. He called the admissions office and told the admissions officer his story. When Rice heard that he was a National Merit Scholar, the school immediately said he was in. Just like that, over the phone. Apparently the president of Rice wanted all the National Merit Scholars he could get. He was intent on beating Harvard and Yale in the National Merit count. So it was a done deal; Myles was going to Rice.

Rice was a strange place even for a person like Myles. The student body was composed of valedictorians, salutatorians, National Merit Scholars, and other equally nerdy men and women. The faculty, largely disgruntled Ivy League wannabes exiled to Texas, tried to avenge their own career frustrations by abusing the smart young people in their classes. During freshman orientation, the university president, the same guy who wanted all these brilliant students to come to his school, told the entering class that a third of them would flunk out and never graduate from Rice.

"Students were regularly having heart attacks, committing suicide, and engaging in other socially unacceptable behavior," Myles told me. "One of my best friends put a rope around his neck, tied the other end of the rope to a bridge railing, and jumped off. Another dove off the Southwest Freeway overpass at Loop 610 into rush hour traffic. A rich kid from California went around stealing petty change from his friends. When he got caught, the school expelled him. I always thought that he hoped that would happen. It was his ticket home."

"Myles, why did students stay if it was so bad? I would have found another place to go. You were all smart."

"Rice was cheap," he said. "William Marsh Rice gave his entire fortune to establish the school and wanted the students to be able to attend free of charge and at one time it had no fees or tuition at all. Students only paid for room and board. By the time I got there, Rice was charging a small tuition, but it was still much cheaper than any comparable school. We stayed there because of the money."

"Are you sorry you stayed?"

Myles thought for a bit then said, "I learned a lot of things at Rice. Unexpected things. Like I found out that experimental physics is just a lot of small-scale, applied engineering projects. You were supposed to devise some apparatus to test a theory. I felt like I was in training to become an upscale auto mechanic.

"Anyway, I did all that when I was building my Soap Box Derby car. I remember being surprised that everyone didn't already know how to do that kind of stuff and that a prestigious university like Rice was wasting time training mechanics. My physics professor told me to quit coming to lab because it was a waste of my time."

"So what did you decide to study?"

"I dropped the labs and began to think about theoretical physics and mathematics. I enjoyed the intellectual challenge but decided that I could not do that for the rest of my life. I was just going to be filling in the blanks on a paint-by-numbers canvas. There had been some recent breakthroughs in describing the fundamental structure of matter, and everyone was busily working out the mathematical details underlying the latest theory.

"You more or less knew what was needed. You just had to do the work," Myles explained. "This takes a lot of brain power, but after a while it's boring. Think of your dentist, probably a pretty smart guy, spending his time looking into people's mouths over and over, day after day, filling cavities. Essentially theoretical scientists filled cavities."

By the end of his junior year, Myles knew two things he didn't want to do. He didn't want to be a physicist, and he didn't want to be a mathematician. But what did he want to do? Where would he go when he left Rice?

"I didn't really find my career path until my senior year. I had decided, on a lark, to take an introductory economics course. I liked the course and the guy teaching the course, Dr. Schwartz, seemed to like the papers I wrote.

"I happened to run into him at Sammy's, the campus coffee shop, just before Thanksgiving. He asked me what I was majoring in and when I told him I was a math/physics double major, he asked what I knew about computers?

"I had worked in the computer lab at General Dynamics the previous summer and felt that I knew about as much as anybody on campus about programming. It turned out that Dr. Schwartz was doing an analysis of census data and needed some computer help. He told me if I were interested in working with him, he could pay me a small salary out of his grant. It sounded good to me, and I began work immediately.

"We were at the computer center late one night during the Christmas break when Dr. Schwartz asked me what I was going to do with myself after I graduated. I had applied to some grad schools in math, but I wasn't that excited about the prospects of being a mathematician. I liked history, politics, sociology, and economics. I told Schwartz that I liked his course a lot, but didn't know what I was going to do.

"Schwartz said that economics departments were looking for people with mathematical backgrounds and that I would fit right into where the profession was headed. He offered to help me make the transition from math to economics if I were interested. He suggested that I stay at Rice two more years to get a master's in economics. If I did well, he would give me a recommendation at his alma mater, Johns Hopkins. So, there in the basement of Garland Hall, at 2:15 in the morning three days after Christmas my senior year, my future was determined."

Myles's second encounter during his senior year involved a girl, a pretty and smart coed who helped him discover that he really enjoyed sex. For most boys, that realization would have come much earlier, but Myles was inexperienced when it came to women. He was a twenty-one-year-old virgin who had gotten his hand inside a few bras but that was it. Anne Ferguson changed that. A freshman from Washington, D.C., Anne was in many ways a classic TRG, a Typical Rice Girl. TRGs were not ugly, but they didn't spend much time worrying about makeup and dressing well. They were smart and ambitious, more interested in pursuing their careers than in pursuing boys. There was a wholesome quality to the TRGs that, after three years of near monastic living, the Typical Rice Boy found attractive.

To make some extra spending money, Myles washed dishes in the cafeteria at Brown College, the all-female dorm where Anne lived. The dishwashers were called "grubs." For reasons that could only be explained by a TRG, the girls considered it an honor to sit at the grub table. One evening Anne and her roommate invited themselves to dine with the grubs. She made sure she sat next to Myles. After introducing herself, she said to Myles, "Don't you grade for Math 101?" Math 101 was the designation for first-year calculus at Rice.

"Sure. I grade for Professor Hemphill. Who do you have?"

Anne already knew that Myles was her math grader, and the purpose of the contact was to solicit some help. "Wow, that's who I have. This week's homework is just killing me. Do you have any time after dinner to help me a little?"

"Sure. I could stay for a while. I have to finish with the dishes first."

Anne told him, "I have reserved study room three. Just come in whenever you are done."

Brown had a series of private study rooms with two desks and a couch. The door closed but didn't lock. Protocol required knocking before entering to give the occupants a chance to move from the couch to the desks. Myles and Anne pretty much had a permanent reservation on study room three for the rest of the semester.

At that time, Rice was known for its wild keg parties. *U.S. News and World Report* had listed it as one of the top ten party schools in the entire country. The Rice Pajama Party, held each year in April, was advertised as "BYOM" meaning bring your own mattress. The event was held in a warehouse, and no furniture was provided so as to accommodate the several hundred mattresses that the students brought with them, mostly from the university dorms. Everyone was supposed to come to the party dressed in pajamas of one sort or another.

After one particularly intense study session, Anne asked Myles, "Want to take me to the Pajama Party next week? I hear it is really crazy."

"I can't say how crazy it is. I've never been. You're supposed to take your mattress, and I don't relish the idea of my mattress getting soaked with beer or something worse."

"Look, you've helped me a lot in math this year, and I need some way to pay you back. This will be my treat. I promise not to spill too much beer on your mattress."

Both Myles's mattress and his date got soaked with beer at the party. On the way home, Myles stopped the car in a remote area of the student parking lot near the track stadium. After sitting for a moment, he put his arm around Anne and kissed her. It was the first time he had passionately kissed anyone. Anne responded in kind, and, after some necking, he moved on to unbutton her pajama top. He could tell she was not wearing anything underneath it. Anne smiled and said, "I was wondering if I was going to have to do that myself." Myles and Anne were married at the end of her junior year, just before heading to Baltimore and Hopkins to start their life together.

After ten years of graduate school and teaching in the mid-Atlantic states, Myles faced a crisis. He had been successful, completing his graduate work and dissertation in near record time. He had been on the faculty at George Washington University in Washington, D.C. for five years and then at the University of Virginia for two. He was an associate professor with tenure, but he wasn't happy. Part of his problem was money. Being a professor doesn't pay that much, unless you are a real star, and he wasn't a star, at least not yet. Part of his problem was being away from Texas. Myles and Anne had two children and another one on the way. He wanted to raise his kids in Texas. When an endowed professorship became available at the University of Houston, Myles took it.

Even though Myles was convinced that he was making the right decision for himself and his family, it was difficult to leave the University of Virginia. Family members and colleagues had a hard time understanding how Myles could leave one of the top five economics departments in the nation for an appointment at a good, but second-tier university. Anne's family in Washington didn't like the grandchildren moving so far away. Anne loved Charlottesville and did not have fond memories of the Houston climate.

All Myles knew was that this is what he wanted. He had been doing things that other people wanted him to do most of his life. To take a stand felt unusual, like jumping off a cliff when a lion was headed toward you: you had to jump but weren't sure what would come next. Doing what others say to do feels much safer. Myles's anxiety level was definitely elevated.

The process of wrapping up his existing responsibilities proved difficult and somewhat painful. The dean at Virginia was angry that Myles was leaving after only two years, especially since he was going to U of H. Tenured appointments involve a difficult, time-consuming process, and the dean felt all his hard work had been for nothing. They almost came to fisticuffs at one point. The dean forced Myles to continue to take part in departmental administrative activities simply to harass him. Myles had already committed to teach an introductory course in economics at the University of Virginia School of Medicine that summer. He had been doing this for a number of years, even before he joined the faculty at UVa, and was expected back again that summer.

On the positive side, Megan Moncrief, a new assistant professor, had agreed to help with the course. She had a PhD from Chicago and was a rising star in the field of medical economics. Her dissertation was on the optimization of medical expenditures at the end of life: How does a person, or society in general, decide how much an additional day or month of life is worth? The analysis involved standard optimization theory but, until now, people had been reluctant to apply impersonal analytic tools to the life and death decisions routinely made in hospitals. Insurance companies and government agencies were increasingly interested in finding a technical justification for cutting off funds to terminally ill patients. Megan was doing groundbreaking research on that topic.

Given that this would be Myles's last summer at Virginia, Megan would likely lead the program the following year. She knew that a good recommendation from Myles would help her get the job. Megan had only been at UVa a year, but Myles knew her pretty well. Each morning at around ten o'clock the economics faculty met for coffee at the faculty club to informally discuss departmental matters and to catch up on each other's personal lives. Megan almost always showed up for coffee and often sat next to Myles.

Megan was an active runner and had run the Chicago Marathon twice when she was in grad school there. At the morning coffees, she had tried to recruit other faculty members to run with her but had had no success. The chairman of the department, a crusty, older gentleman, once voiced the opinion of many of his colleagues, "Ms. Moncrief, running is a waste of time. We are here to do research, write, and publish, not to traipse around the campus in our underwear." Megan took the hint.

One morning in late April, on the way back to their offices, Megan asked, "Myles, since we're going to be teaching that class over at the med school, why don't we start running together? A morning run would be the perfect time to discuss plans for the course. We could get some exercise in, and you could tell me about what you have in mind for the program."

It did seem like a good idea to Myles. "Okay, but you will have to take it slow. I'm in horrible shape. I don't know if I can run two blocks without resting."

"No problem. I will meet you tomorrow morning at six on University Avenue in front of the Rotunda."

By the time the semester ended, Myles and Anne had sold their Charlottesville home and were due to close on it July 9th. Anne and the kids would then head to Houston, but Myles would have to stay an extra week in Charlottesville to finish his teaching commitment. On a run, Myles mentioned to Megan, "I am lookin' for a place to stay after we sell our house. Do you know anyone who is out of town for the summer? All I need is a place to crash for a week."

"Why don't you stay with me? I have an apartment with two bedrooms. I use the second bedroom as a study, but it has a foldout couch that you could use. It's not all that comfortable, but for a week maybe it will be okay."

Myles was reluctant to stay with a female colleague. He knew the departmental gossip mill would be running full steam when word got around that he was living with Megan—even if it was just for a week. "Let me see what Anne thinks. Thanks for the offer."

At dinner that evening, Myles told Anne about Megan's offer, "It would certainly be the easiest thing to do, but I feel weird about it."

"Are you worried about what the department secretaries will say?" Anne asked.

"No, I don't care what anybody at school thinks. I just don't want you to be upset. That's all."

"Myles, I know you too well to worry about any hanky-panky between you two. It sounds like a good idea to me."

Anne's mother and father arrived in Charlottesville on the Fourth of July to help pack up and drive Anne and the kids to Houston. Mrs. Ferguson nearly went ballistic when she found out Myles was spending the week at Megan's. She told Anne, "You should stay here and guard your property. I've met Megan, and she is a cute little thing. Myles seemed awfully friendly with her. They're going to end up in bed together."

Anne said, "Mom, don't be ridiculous. If they were going to do anything, they could do it whether Myles was staying with her or not. Anyway, you don't know how backward Myles is when it comes to women. Take my word for it, he won't try anything."

Anne, the kids, and her parents headed for Houston on Friday. The movers came on the following Sunday. After supervising the loading of their stuff and cleaning up the house, Myles moved into Megan's apartment with enough clothes to last the week.

Monday morning Myles and Megan headed out for their run as usual. Coming home they walked the last few blocks back to Megan's place in order to cool off and catch their breath. Megan said, "Thanks for running with me these last few weeks."

"I've enjoyed it a lot more than I expected. I may keep running when I get to Houston, if I can stand the heat and the humidity."

"It's been great getting to know you better, but I really wanted to have you along for protection."

The neighborhood around campus was somewhat sketchy, but Myles had never considered any place in Charlottesville really dangerous. He asked, "Why do you need protection?"

Megan said, "Because of these."

He looked over at her and saw that she was holding up her bosoms, one in each hand.

Megan continued, "Guys tend to yell at me from cars, honk their horns, or simply come over to get a better look. With you along, the jerks haven't bothered me, and I was able to relax and enjoy my runs. That was why I was trying to get some other faculty members to run with me. I couldn't very well have explained the real reason I wanted a running companion at our morning coffees."

Myles and Megan had had nothing but a close collegial relationship, so he was a bit startled by this personal information. Even though they spent a lot of time together, there was never a hint of anything sexual. Myles was ten years older than Megan, and he considered himself to be her mentor. Now she was holding her boobs out for him to see. They were covered by a sports bra, but still it seemed inappropriate. Frankly, he didn't think they were anything special. He hadn't really noticed them before. Now, he wasn't sure what would happen when they got back to the apartment. All he could think to say was, "Oh, I see."

There was only one bathroom in Megan's apartment. Megan told Myles, "You get first shower. I'll set out some cereal and milk for breakfast."

Myles had barely started showering when the door to the bathroom opened and Megan stepped into the room wearing only a towel. "Are you going to take all day?"

"Sorry. I'll be done in a minute."

Dropping her towel and climbing into the shower, Megan replied, "No problem."

Megan's breasts were nice, but they weren't *Playboy* bunny big, and certainly they were no bigger than Anne's, even before the two children. Megan handed Myles the soap and a washcloth and asked, "Would you wash my back?" He complied. After a couple of minutes, she said, "Turn around. It's your turn." He again complied. Once his back was good and soapy, he could feel Megan pressing against him as she reached around to clean his front. Myles was embarrassed by the response of his body to all this soap and skin and rubbing, but he couldn't control it. When Megan decided he was clean enough, she said matter-of-factly, "It's time to get ready for class."

For the rest of the day, Megan acted as if nothing had happened. She was giving the lectures that week, and Myles was to observe her and report to the faculty on whether or not she was ready to take on the class next year. Myles certainly observed her. What he had seen that morning continued to run through his mind as Megan stood at the blackboard. At lunch she was her normal, collegial self. After work, they walked back to her apartment, and Megan prepared a simple supper of canned tomato soup and tuna sandwiches.

When it came time for bed, Myles asked, "Where are the sheets and pillow for the couch? I'll go ahead and make up my bed."

Megan told him, "There's no reason for you to sleep on the couch.

We already know what each other looks like. We can share my bed. It will be a lot more comfortable than the couch."

Myles had dozed off by the time Megan came to bed. She slid over next to him and put her head on his shoulder. He reached out and pulled her closer. She was naked. Myles could smell her perfume and her shampoo. Her skin was cool and smooth. Their mouths found each other in the darkness as Myles ran his hands up and down her back. Their bodies seemed to just click together. Megan was moving rhythmically against him. He totally forgot where he was and who he was with. Lost in the moment, he finally collapsed, totally spent.

When the alarm went off on Tuesday morning, Megan was spooned against Myles, who had his arms wrapped around her. As she reached for the alarm, he pulled her close to him and nuzzled her hair and neck, but Megan said, "It's time to go for our run."

This pattern was repeated each day for the rest of the week: a run and a shower in the morning followed by a day of work, dinner, and, in the evening, an early bedtime. Neither one of them said anything about it. Neither one of them mentioned "love" or suggested that they had a future after this week. They just did it. On Friday afternoon, after Myles had gathered his things together and loaded his car, Megan gave him a long kiss and said, "Keep running!"

Driving to Houston, Myles realized that he had been unfaithful to Anne. She was the first and, before this week, the only woman he had been intimate with. He always thought of sex as something special that was supposed to occur within a loving relationship that either involved marriage or led to marriage. It was a manifestation of an emotional bond between a man and a woman. It was not a simple physical act like eating or going to the bathroom.

Furthermore, he was especially surprised that a woman like Megan would be willing to engage in sexual activity outside of the marriage bond. He knew, of course, that some of his colleagues had had affairs with students and with each other. One coed at George Washington ended up pregnant as a result of an affair with a prominent political science professor. Another colleague got a new wife every time he decided to write a new book. He often looked no further than the departmental women, female colleagues, or the wives of colleagues, for his new spouse.

Anne hadn't been shy about taking her clothes off, but he thought that was just because she was in love with him. Maybe, if he was a little more open to the possibility, there were other women out there who just wanted sex. Some of the girls in his micro-economics course at UVa had baked cookies for him. One had invited him to come to her sorority house for a party on Easters Weekend, the drunken orgy that was held each year in the spring. All this, on top of moving, was indeed confusing.

Myles continued to run when he got to Houston, and he soon found his way into the Flyers, where we met. He was a slow runner, but he was diligent in his efforts, rarely missing a training session. He liked to tell people about his academic credentials and his experiences on the East Coast. I enjoyed his stories and often made a point of running with him. I don't know how many people heard his "Megan story," but he wasn't shy about telling it.

In Houston, after his experience with Megan, Myles acted more like a ladies man than a nerdy professor. He joked that all running chicks were "hot to trot," so to speak, and constantly flirted with the women runners making suggestive remarks. After a particularly difficult training run, one woman observed, "That was long and hard this morning."

Myles replied, "I thought you liked 'em long and hard."

Another time we had watermelon when we got back to the park. Myles went around asking random female runners, "Do you spit or swallow?" When they blushed, he would explain that he was talking about the watermelon seeds.

While the women had taken offense when Kurt made similar off-color remarks, they apparently had no problem when Myles did so. In fact, many of them sought out his company and liked to run with him. The guys, of course, enjoyed hearing about his purported conquests of coeds at the University of Houston. No question about it, he was a popular guy.

Chapter 5
SUE

Sue came from an athletic family. Her dad, Red Ward, played baseball at Rice and might have played major league ball if the Korean War had not intervened. He got the nickname "Red" because he always carried a red handkerchief with him. He was a short, wiry guy who got into fights with the bigger boys at school. The red handkerchief was supposed to hide the blood so his mother wouldn't know that he had been fighting again. It was a trademark that he continued to carry throughout his life.

After the Army was done with him, Red gave up on his dream to play professional baseball. Instead, he earned a master's degree in physical education from Columbia University in New York City and started his career as a high school coach. In fact, he was the athletic director for the school system in Coshocton, Ohio.

Banky Clifton, Sue's mother, played basketball in high school in West Lafayette, Ohio. Her real name was Margaret, but the girls at school all called her Banky because she liked to bank her shots off the backboard. Banky was the star of her six-woman team. There were few opportunities for girls to play sports in college at that time, so at Ohio State, she played intramural volleyball on a team that managed to come in second her senior year. Red met Banky when she applied to teach physical education in Coshocton. She was pretty and seemed qualified. Red offered her a job, and she accepted.

Banky's family still lived on their farm in West Lafayette, just seven miles from Coshocton. Soon Red and Banky were regulars at the Clifton house. Banky told anyone who asked that she was just being nice to Red because he was so far from his home in Texas. Anyway, Banky had a boyfriend whom she had dated since the sixth grade. Everyone knew Banky and her longtime beau would eventually get married. Red just provided good entertainment with his stories about the Texas frontier.

At the end of her first year of teaching, Banky's boyfriend married a woman from Cleveland. That sent a shock through the small West Lafayette community. Several people thought it was pretty underhanded of him to keep Banky "on the line for so long and then abandon her."

At the same time, Red announced that he was moving back to Houston. His father, a well-connected banker there, was financing a new oil company. The owner wanted Red to manage the company's field operations. The new job paid three times the salary he was receiving as athletic director, and Red had had enough of the Ohio winters. Banky had never been to Texas, but she told Red she wanted to go with him. They were married six weeks later and headed south.

Red and Banky had three children: twin boys, William Robert and Joseph Robert, and Sue, who came along four years after the twins. William and Joseph were names passed down through Red's family; Robert was Banky's brother's name. Banky insisted that her sons were not to be called Billy Bob and Joe Bob. Those were redneck, southern names, and she was still a daughter-of-the-Mayflower Yankee at heart. Sue was named after her great-grandmother Susan Cook of Bridge of Allan, Scotland.

From as early as she could recall, Sue attended her brothers' games. They were both star players in football, basketball, and baseball. Billy went to college on a baseball scholarship and was drafted his junior year to play major league baseball. But he never got to play professional sports; he broke his arm during his senior year. When he graduated, Billy landed a job coaching high school baseball and football in a small town near Amarillo. He couldn't believe people would pay you to coach high school ball. It was just too much fun. Joe was on the college golf team. He didn't make the professional golf circuit, but he did work as a golf pro for a few years before he started selling insurance to the businessmen he had met on the links.

When Red wasn't at one of the boys' games, he would watch a game on TV and, at the same time, listen to one on the radio. It didn't much matter what was being broadcast so long as it was sports. Red's idea of a perfect Saturday was golf until noon, drink a few beers in the clubhouse, catch a Little League game in the afternoon, then watch a game on the tube in the evening. It just didn't get much better than that.

Sue realized early on that if she was going to get any attention from her mom and dad she would have to do something athletic. Banky enrolled Sue in dance at an early age, but Red didn't like to go to dance recitals. He didn't consider dance to be a real athletic event. Sue's dance teacher suggested she take up tumbling. Sue really took to tumbling. There were team competitions, and Red was willing to go to those when the boys didn't have a game. Sue's tumbling skills helped to get her elected cheerleader in high school.

Sue followed in her father's footsteps to Rice. Unlike her father though, she had not expected to be on any of Rice's sports teams. Rice required all freshmen to take a full year of P.E., and the women's track coach was in charge of Sue's P.E. class for the fall semester. She could see that Sue was a natural athlete and invited her to try out for the track team. Sue made the team in the one-mile and two-mile events. She was not the star runner for Rice, but to be on the team was enough for her. In Sue's mind, she had finally equaled her brothers' achievements. Red loved to come to his alma mater to watch his daughter compete. A few of his classmates from the old days regularly came to the track meets, and Red bragged about Sue's running.

On the first day of classes, Sue sat next to a pudgy short guy who looked about twelve years old. Sue stuck her hand out and said, "I'm Sue Ward."

The boy responded, "My name is Lloyd Landerman."

"Nice to meet you, Lloyd. What are you going to major in?"

"Don't know. Haven't decided yet. Might be math, might be physics, might be chemistry. I'm pretty good in all of them."

"I'm definitely going to major in math. I want to be a high school math teacher, maybe at Bellaire High School. That's where I went. Where did you go to high school?"

"I went to Highland Park. You know, up in Dallas. My father is on the faculty at Southwestern Medical School. Maybe I'll be a doctor, too."

Lloyd was exotic to Sue. He was so different from the men in her family and the boys she had known in high school. In the first place, Lloyd was, indeed, a year younger than the other freshmen. He had skipped his last year of high school. And Lloyd was a nerd with no athletic ability and he was proud of it. He didn't play golf or tennis. He didn't hunt or fish. He didn't like to watch sports on television or listen to the Astros on the radio. He didn't even go to the Rice football games when they were less than a quarter mile away and free. Lloyd liked to study. Lloyd liked to think. Lloyd liked to discuss important ideas. He once set up some seats in his dorm room and invited the football team to come watch him study.

Lloyd was awed by Sue's beauty and her athletic ability. He deviated from his longstanding disdain for sporting events in order to attend her track meets. He even occasionally watched her workouts. Lloyd and Red became good buddies as they cheered for Sue and the rest of the Rice team. Sue liked to think of Lloyd as the little brother she never had. Her friends called him her puppy dog. They were not a couple, and Sue dated other guys. She could tell that it bothered Lloyd, but he never asked her out.

By the time he was a senior, Lloyd's career plans had changed. He had decided to go to law school at the University of Texas. He had matured a lot at Rice and had outgrown his infatuation with science. Graduating magna cum laude, Lloyd easily made it into Texas. He was on the *Law Review* there and graduated number three in his law class. He had a lot of the big name law firms chasing after him, and Lloyd decided to go with Vinson and Elkins, working in the firm's Houston energy practice.

When Lloyd moved back to Houston, he gave Red a call. Red had good business connections, and Lloyd wanted to begin to develop contacts with potential clients. Red and Lloyd met for lunch at the Petroleum Club at the top of the Exxon Building in downtown. It was where the movers and shakers of the Houston business community did big dollar deals. Lloyd asked politely about the family including Sue. Joe was still in Dallas but William, as he was now called, was living in Atlanta coaching for the Braves. He evaluated high school and college prospects and worked with the young players to help ease their transition into the ranks of professional baseball. Sue was in Houston. She was still unmarried. Red suggested that Lloyd give her a call.

Like all young associate attorneys, Lloyd was working ridiculous hours. He did not have much time for socializing, but he did call Sue. Lloyd's law firm had tickets to the opera, and he asked Sue to go with him. Still as pretty as ever, Sue was happy with her life. She was teaching math at the Bellaire High School, her alma mater, and was still running, not competitively, but still running. She had a date now and then, but she really liked hanging out with a couple of girls that she ran with and her dog, Rufus, a springer spaniel. She had recently joined a marathon training program, the Memorial Park Flyers.

Sue enjoyed the simple pleasures of life: her dog, her work, running, watching TV, Mexican restaurants, and working in the yard. Lloyd enjoyed the opera and symphony, fancy restaurants, sophisticated people, and work. He really liked the challenge of litigation. He hoped to make partner at V&E, and he was one of the few young lawyers not intimidated by the selection process. In spite of these differences, on some level, they connected. Maybe, in some mystical way, they completed each other. They began going out at least once a week and even took a vacation to New York on Labor Day weekend.

Lloyd began to think about marriage. The partners that Lloyd worked with at Vinson and Elkins were married, and they had told him that a wife was useful in a successful law practice. You needed a hostess for your parties and someone to make connections in the charity circuit. Sue was the only girl he knew very well. He started hinting around about getting married. Sue's family was also encouraging her to push things forward. Lloyd didn't fit into the sporting lifestyle of the family, but he was successful. He was likely to become one of the richest men in Houston. They thought he would make a good son-in-law. When Lloyd finally proposed, Sue accepted.

Lloyd bought a house in Bellaire close to the school where Sue taught. It was a newly built mansion on a half acre of land. It was plenty big for entertaining and raising a family. Both Sue and Lloyd wanted to have children, but things didn't seem to work out. The doctors said that there was a problem with the quality of Sue's eggs. They didn't rule out pregnancy but said it would be unlikely. Sue and Lloyd thought about adopting. Their options were limited: severely distressed older children or infants from China or Russia. Lloyd was not interested in a foreign adoption. The next step would be to try in vitro fertilization, maybe with a donor egg.

Lloyd made partner and was busier than ever. He seldom was home in time for dinner and was out of town a lot. Sue increasingly focused on her running. Kurt, the owner of the Flyers, asked her to serve as an assistant coach, and as a teacher, she readily took to helping inexperienced runners finish a marathon. She liked getting out of the house and being around other runners. She was lonely. The Flyers became her family.

When Sue's father retired, her parents moved to Huntsville, a small college town seventy miles north of Houston. They had a house on the golf course at Elkins Lake, a planned development that was nestled in a pine forest surrounding a small lake. It had originally been the country home of Judge Elkins, the founder of Lloyd's law firm. Judge Elkins' manor house now served as a clubhouse and restaurant for the residents of the community.

Banky and Red organized a family get together each October in conjunction with the Fair on the Square, an old-fashioned harvest festival held each year at the courthouse in downtown Huntsville. Their two sons had already committed to bringing their families for the weekend. The men were going to play golf and watch football. The women would take the children into town to visit the fair. Banky called Sue to remind her about the fair that weekend.

"Mom, I don't know if we are going to make it this year," Sue told her mother.

"I thought you might want to run in the race they hold on Saturday morning. We have been having great weather."

"That does sound like fun. I have a marathon in three weeks, and I could run in the shorter race as a warmup. Let me see what Lloyd has to say."

She knew that Lloyd wouldn't want to go, but the race sounded interesting to her, so she went ahead and asked, "How about going up to Mom and Dad's for the weekend? Everybody's coming into town. I don't get to see my whole family that often."

"Sue, you know I have a trial starting in two weeks, and at the moment the whole case is going to hell in a hand basket. Yesterday, the judge granted their motion *in limine* and now I've got to retool our entire defense strategy," Lloyd told Sue. "Anyway, I don't play golf, and I'm sure not going to sit around in front of the TV drinking beer all weekend."

"There is a race there I want to run Saturday morning. We could drive up early Saturday. I would run the Fair on the Square race. Then, everyone could go to lunch at the Manor House, and after lunch we could come home."

"I have a bad feeling about this. Your family never sticks to an agenda. I need to be back here by three o'clock."

"Everything will be over up there by two. We should be able to get back by around three."

The Fair on the Square Race featured a quarter marathon and a half marathon. The course was out and back so runners could turn around at three and a quarter miles for the quarter marathon or at six and a half miles for the half marathon. Sue had been running pretty well and felt good about her upcoming Chicago Marathon. Furthermore, the weatherman forecast perfect running conditions, and for once, the forecast was right. The only challenge was going to be the hills. While Houston is totally, completely, positively flat, Huntsville is quite hilly. She had decided to run the quarter marathon, which was only six and a half miles. "That's barely more than a 10K," Sue told herself.

Sue started off strong, and, as the race progressed, she began to think, "Why waste a great run? I'll go for the half." She was supposed to be tapering for Chicago. The previous weekend she had run twenty-one miles. Her schedule called for shorter runs during the next two weeks in order to rest and prepare for running the 26.2 miles she would face in the marathon. At the turnaround point for the quarter marathon, she was feeling really good. Ignoring the advice she had just given to the runners she coached, she soldiered on, not realizing that the reason it seemed so easy was that she had been going downhill since the start.

Sue made it to the half marathon turnaround point and was beginning to think she had made a mistake. Lloyd was waiting at the finish line expecting her back an hour after the start. She had not brought her cell phone with her so he would be wondering where she was. She felt like she needed to get back as quickly as possible.

The run back was misery. Miles six to nine had a slight upgrade, but from the nine mile marker to the finish the course shot uphill with a nasty climb the last half mile. It was the hardest Sue ever ran, before or since. She didn't walk, though her legs were calling out for relief. She was in pain, but she kept pushing. Sue crossed under the clock at the finish line in one hour and forty-one minutes. That time put her in the top quarter of all women her age in America in the half marathon. For someone who was supposed to be taking it easy, it was an impressive result.

Sue could not feel her pelvic girdle. Everything below her waist was numb. She needed help standing. Lloyd carried her over to a picnic table where she laid down to rest while he went to get the car. He had to help her stumble to the car. His first words were, "Where have you been? I've been standing here for almost two hours waiting for you. You told me you would finish in less than an hour." Sue didn't say anything, but she knew there was going to be trouble.

The lunch was also delayed. Lloyd's in-laws didn't finish their round of golf until one o'clock. By the time everyone finally got to the Manor House, it was close to two o'clock. Sue recounted each painful step of her run that morning. She basked in Red's praise in front of her brothers. It was as if they were back at the Rice track stadium and she had just won a race. Lloyd said little during the meal. He was not happy to be there in the first place, he was not happy that he had to wait on Sue to finish, he was not happy to have lunch delayed, and he was not happy that Sue would be going to Chicago for the marathon.

When they finally got into the car and headed back to Houston it was four o'clock. Both Lloyd and Sue were silent on the ride home. Neither one wanted to argue. Lloyd had learned a long time ago that it was useless to argue with his wife. Any agreement that came out of the argument was good for about ten seconds. Sue liked to be spontaneous; it was part of her charm. She decided at the last minute to do the half marathon that morning without thinking about all the implications of that decision. It was just no use trying to plan anything with her because she never stuck to the plan. It was already well past five o'clock, and they weren't home yet.

Sue didn't like to argue with Lloyd because he was too good at it. After all, he was one of the highest paid arguers in the state of Texas. His positions always seemed logical, and usually she could not come up with good reasons as to why he was wrong. He always wanted to plan everything out ahead of time. Lloyd was too controlling; he expected her to stick to the plan that he had designed. She felt it was best to avoid arguments or to quickly give in. She could still do whatever she wanted to do when the time came.

Finally Lloyd said, "You have to quit."

Sue asked, "What do you mean I have to quit? I have to quit what?"

"You have to quit running. It takes too much time, and it is too hard on your body," Lloyd responded. "I thought I was going to have to take you to the emergency room this morning. That would have made it the perfect day for sure."

Sue was too tired to fight about unimportant things, but no way in hell was she going to quit running. Running was the most important thing in her life at the moment. She told Lloyd, "You know how I much I love running. Besides, all of my friends are runners. No way can I quit."

"That's another thing," Lloyd said. "Those runners are all fruitcakes. I don't know why you would want to be around that bunch of losers."

Sue had heard this before, and she was tempted to tell Lloyd that he needed to get some new lines. Instead she said, "Well, if you were ever home, then maybe I would have someone to do things with."

"Sue, you know the kind of hours lawyers have to work. You don't seem to mind the big house and fancy cars that come along with my job. Long hours are just part of the territory."

When Sue failed to respond, he added, "You shouldn't go to Chicago. You have totally blown your training. No way can you have a good time there after what you did to yourself today." Sue remained silent.

These fights had become so scripted that neither party needed to continue to know where this one was headed. They had been over this ground many times. Lloyd knew that he was an absent husband, but he was doing it, at least in part, for them. Maybe if they had kids, Sue would be able to see that. Sue liked having the money and knew that the hours were necessary. For better or worse, it was the deal they had struck. Both were silent the rest of the way back to Bellaire.

When Lloyd pulled off the freeway at their exit, Sue said calmly, "Lloyd, I don't want to argue anymore. I'm simply too tired. I am not going to stop running, and I am going to Chicago."

Chapter 6

NICK

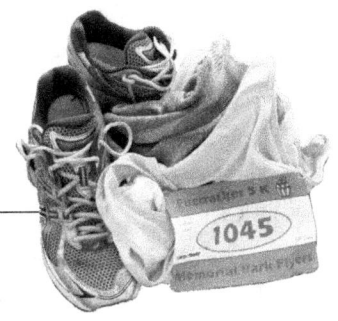

Nick was a strong, fast runner. Besides his job as the head administrative nurse in the cardiac unit at Methodist Hospital, running was his only activity. He had never married and lived by himself. He spent most of his free time training. Although I was too slow to run with him, we became good friends, and he loved to tell me about his family background, which was an unusual amalgam of Missouri hillbillies and Russian immigrants. One might say that Nick was the product of the great American melting pot.

His father was born and raised on a forty-acre rock farm in the hills of southwestern Missouri. The nearest town, Neosho, was eighteen miles away. Water was lifted in a bucket from a hand-dug well, and baths were taken one night a week outside in a horse trough. A big black kettle over an open fire was used to heat water for clothes washing. Ashes from the fire were saved to make lye soap or sprinkle in the outhouse to keep the smell down. The Sears catalog served as toilet paper.

Nick's great grandmother Becky Schiesman was a hard-cussing, tobacco-chewing, gun-toting frontier woman who, as a young girl, had served coffee to the James Boys when they passed through southwestern Missouri. According to family legend, no electricity was allowed in the house because, having once been struck by lightning, she could feel it flowing through her. She found divorce too cumbersome a process and took to running her men off with a shotgun when she had had enough of them.

Nick's grandmother, Ethel, was born on the farm and later married Dudley Lebow. Ethel and Dudley kept the farm when Becky passed away and eked out a living by raising a few cows and selling milk and eggs. Occasionally Dudley would do odd jobs in Neosho when they needed a little extra money. Mostly the Lebows were outside of the cash economy and had to do for themselves. Their son Andrew, later to become Nick's father, was the first one in the family to be born in a hospital.

When Andy, as everyone but his mother called him, graduated from high school, he was immediately drafted into the Army. It was 1942 and the nation was at war. All able-bodied young men were asked to serve, and you didn't get too much choice as to where you were assigned or what your army job was. Because of his work on the farm, Andy was familiar with engines and tools having frequently repaired the family's old '31 Ford Model A. He also helped his father maintain the house, the barn, and the assorted machinery that was necessary to operate a working farm. Based on this experience, he was assigned to the motor pool and deployed to England. There he learned how to work on a wide variety of equipment but was eventually assigned to the 66th Armored Regiment that landed in France, three days after D-Day. The march to Berlin was relatively quick, and, except for occasional German sniper fire, he was rarely in harm's way.

After the war, Andy's story was a familiar one: "How ya gonna keep 'em down on the farm, after they've seen Paree?" Andy had no desire to go back to Neosho and a life of subsistence farming. His cousin, Johnny Schiesman, lived in Sioux City, Iowa. Johnny said there were plenty of jobs there. Andy decided to give Sioux City a try.

Ideally situated on the east side of the Missouri River, Sioux City had grown rapidly as refrigerated railcars allowed livestock to be slaughtered in the west, closer to the cattle ranches and feedlots, and then shipped east. By 1940, Sioux City was a major railroad hub and the fourth largest packing center behind Chicago, Kansas City, and Omaha. The stockyards covered more than four hundred acres and could be smelled from anywhere in town. The locals liked to say that it was the "smell of money."

In the first decades of the twentieth century, immigrants poured into Sioux City from Poland, Russia, and Lithuania to work for Swift, Amour, Cudahy, and other meatpackers. Recently arrived ethnic groups found homes in the "South Bottoms," living close to the Missouri River on the south side of the stockyards. These people were peasants, fresh from the villages of Eastern Europe. They were just learning English and had separate churches for their national religions and separate grocery stores where their language was spoken and food from their home countries was available.

When Andy arrived in Sioux City, he quickly found a job working on the killing floor at Swift. The cows were lined up in a chute and, one by one, as they arrived at the enclosed platform where Andy stood, he hit them on the head with a large sledge hammer. He then released the platform, and the stunned cow dropped to the floor below where it was hoisted up by its hind legs to an overhead conveyor and its throat slit. As it bled to death, it was skinned and the disassembly process started.

Life in the packing plants was rough. It was not uncommon for men to settle their differences wrestling on the catwalk over the rendering vat: the loser ending up in the boiling fat below. One time, Andy saw a fellow purposefully drop a cow to the killing floor without stunning it first. The guy just wanted to see what would happen.

The women's job was to trim meat off bones for sausage and lunch meats. Seated on both sides of a long cutting table, the women wielded ten-inch long butcher knives sharpened like razors. As the bones fell from the conveyor belt above the women, knife fights would break out over choice pieces.

Andy's cousin had married Tonya Morski, a cute Russian girl with blonde hair and a nice figure. Tonya was pretty and outgoing, a real good-time girl. Johnny and Tonya usually had Sunday dinner at her parents' place where the menu featured Russian dishes including cabbage rolls, homemade kielbasa, sautéed mushrooms, and sticky chicken. It was accompanied by dark rye bread from Heime's Bakery and some sweet red wine made from last season's grapes.

The Morskis' home was in immaculate condition. It was painted yellow with gray trim. A high picket fence surrounded the property. The street was not paved, but there was a yellow log lying in front of the house serving as a curb and demarcating the property line. From there, a sidewalk led through a gate up to the large front porch with room for two rocking chairs and a couch.

Tonya had an older brother, Nicholas, and a younger sister, Larisa, who were usually present at the family Sunday dinners. Nicholas and Tonya had the round faces that one often associates with Russians, while Larisa was thin with an angular, chiseled face. She projected that emaciated WASP look that was popular in Hollywood. Her dark reddish hair was bobbed with a tight perm. She often carried a Lucky Strike in her tortoiseshell cigarette holder.

Soon after he arrived, Andy was invited to have Sunday dinner with Tonya's family. He enjoyed the exotic food and the family table talk, but mostly he was smitten by Larisa. He thought she was the prettiest woman he had ever seen. Andy and Larisa began going to movies and meeting for picnics in Stone Park.

Andy thought that Larisa was special. She was totally different than the girls he knew back in the hills of Missouri. She reminded him more of the women he had met in France. He soon decided that he wanted her to be his wife. After one Sunday dinner, Larisa and Andy were sitting on the front porch talking about the upcoming week.

Larisa had just taken a job at Davidson's, one of the two large department stores in Sioux City. It was her first job since she graduated from high school. She explained to Andy, "I can't go to the movies on Tuesday or Thursday for a while. I have to stay after the store closes to straighten the displays and put out new clothes. Maybe I can move into sales after a while."

"I know they will want you out on the floor soon. Anyway, maybe next Saturday you can help me find a place of my own. It's kind of cramped at Johnny and Tonya's apartment."

"Where would you move?" Larisa asked.

"I'm not sure. I need your help to pick a place. There is an apartment available over on Villa Avenue. It's close to Johnny's. It needs to be big enough for two people."

"Why do you need room for two? Are you going to get a roommate?"

"I was thinking that you and I might—well, we might team up. You know, get married."

Before answering, Larisa went into the house and came out with a pack of cigarettes. After lighting one and taking a couple of puffs, she said, "Andy, you are a swell guy, but I have ambitions. I want to get ahead. I am not sure you want to do that."

Andy thought she would readily say yes and was taken aback by her answer. "I do want to get ahead. I came here to get away from the farm—to make my fortune."

"But you're just knockin' cows in the head. What kind of fortune is that? Nicky is going to college on the GI Bill and is going to become a lawyer. The government is paying for it. You could do that, too."

"Yes, but Nicky went to Central High here in a big city. My high school class had seven people in it. I don't think I could make it in college."

"Well, Johnny and Tonya are going to start a bakery over in Morningside. They have plans."

Andy didn't really understand what Larisa wanted, so he asked, "What are your plans, Larisa? What do you want to do?"

"I want to get away from Sioux City. I want to go where people don't know I am a Russian immigrant from the South Bottoms. Did Tonya tell you about what happened when she was elected cheerleader at Central?"

"No. I am not surprised she got elected. She is real pretty and a lot of fun."

"Yah, she was elected but the principal told her that 'No Russian bitch from the Bottoms was going to represent the Central High School so long as he was in charge.' I have to get away from that."

"For me Sioux City is a big deal. I enjoy living here, having a little money to spend, and being with you. I haven't given much thought to what comes next. But what I need to know is: do you love me?"

"Yes, Andy, I love you. I love you a lot. I just can't stay here in Sioux City married to someone who works at the packing plant."

"I love you, Larisa, more than anything. I want you to be my wife. Let me think about where we could go, about what I could do."

Andy had an army buddy from the motor pool whose family owned a Chevy dealership in Wichita, Kansas. The guy had told Andy if he ever needed a job, he could come work for them. Andy knew he was a good mechanic, and before long, he had lined up a job in Wichita in his buddy's auto garage. When he told Larisa about his plan, she said, "That is a good start. Of course, you wouldn't want to be a grease monkey all your life, but it gets us out of Sioux City."

Wichita was fine with Larisa. It was close enough to Iowa to make family visits easy but far enough away that no one would have to know about her background. Also there were a lot of opportunities in Wichita. The aircraft industry had rapidly expanded during the Second World War as plants were built by Boeing, Cessna, Lockheed, and Beechcraft. She was sure that Andy could get ahead there, and this time she said, "Yes."

People react to humble beginnings in different ways. Some are proud of starting life poor; others try to hide common beginnings, putting on airs. Larisa took the latter route. She was determined to be perceived as a cultured person with style. She did not want people to know that her parents were immigrants, that her mother had worked in the packing house, and that her father worked night shifts at the railyard. It was not exactly that she was ashamed or embarrassed by her family so much as she just didn't want that to be her identity.

Andy, on the other hand, was proud of his hillbilly background. Proud that he could shoot, fight, fix an engine, and build a house. He didn't need the luxuries of life. He was not particularly impressed with them. He once drew the Lebow family seal, claiming to have found it in some old papers at the farm. His "seal" contained the Stars and Bars, a plow, and a tomahawk. He always told people that his grandfather was a full-blood Cherokee. The farther he had to come, the better he felt about himself.

Even though Larisa and Andy loved each other, this difference in attitude would define their marriage and have a profound impact on their children. "My mother was always trying to keep up with and get ahead of the Joneses," Nick said. "She had a flair for entertaining and decorating. She enjoyed hosting dinner parties where she served fancy appetizers and exotic cocktails. There were paintings on the walls in our house, and classical music could often be heard on the phonograph. She was always dressed in fashionable clothes compared to the other women in the neighborhood."

One of the things Nick came to understand was that Tracy, his older sister, was Larisa's hope for the future. Nine years older than Nick, Tracy was going to be a ballerina or a musician or an artist. Larisa decorated the house, chose clothing, and decided which church to attend in order to groom Tracy for the big future that she planned for her. Larisa often talked at dinner about New York and Hollywood, though she had actually never been to either place. Tracy, on the other hand, never seemed too interested in a career in show business.

Nick and his family regularly attended Tracy's performances, and he resented that. His attitude was like that of many younger siblings forced to attend performances given by older brothers and sisters: The shows were boring. At one Tracy was supposed to be doing a harem dance. As she spun around, she got tangled in the painted sheet that hung behind the stage and pulled it, and herself, to the floor. She was rescued from too much embarrassment because precisely at that moment someone entered the auditorium shouting that the younger brother of another girl on stage had just been hit by a car. The boy had slipped out of the auditorium and was trying to get to the park across the street. There was a lot of blood, and the rest of the show was cancelled.

One Thanksgiving, when Nick was eight years old, Uncle Nicholas and his family were visiting from Dallas where Nicholas had built a successful family law practice. Tracy was scheduled to entertain the family by playing the marimba. A marimba is like a xylophone except the keys are wooden and there are tubes protruding under the keys to amplify the sound. It is an ancient instrument, but one rarely played anymore. Like accordions, its place has been taken by electric synthesizers that can produce similar sounds much more easily.

While Tracy played her marimba high above his head, Nick sat squirming on the floor making faces and punching his cousin in the ear. Finally, his mother had had enough. She stopped the music and told Nick, "You are being very rude to all of us. I am trying to introduce you to a few of the finer things in life. I don't want my son to grow up to be ignorant and uncultured. And to behave that way in front of your uncle Nicholas, who, I will remind you, you were named after, is so embarrassing."

Nick responded, "Playing a marimba is dumb. I don't see why I have to be here."

Larisa launched a rolled-up magazine in Nick's direction. He ducked. The magazine hit a table breaking a souvenir tea cup and saucer that Andy had bought for Larisa on a Lions Club trip to Chicago. Now the screaming really started. "You naughty boy, look what you have done," his mother said barely restraining her tears. "Get out of here. I have had enough of you. You managed to spoil our whole Thanksgiving Day."

Nick got up, walked out of the house, and began running around their small backyard. Nick didn't know why he was running. He simply had to escape. He was not running fast, just a slow jog around the perimeter of the yard. Except for playing with his friends, Nick had never had any interest in running. In retrospect, he thinks it must have been the innate "fight or flight" response to a crisis. He had tried fighting and now he was running.

After about ten minutes, Larisa came out and asked, "Just what do you think you are doing?"

"I'm running."

"I can see that. Don't hurt yourself. You've already caused enough trouble today."

After ten more minutes, Nick was tired and came back inside the house. Larisa had calmed down by then, and Nick was sure that his bizarre behavior had somewhat bamboozled the adults. From that day on, Nick knew that he would be a runner.

In talking about this defining event in his life, Nick told me, "I now realize that my mom was so upset because things were not working out for Tracy. She was, in fact, not very talented and not a very good student. She only had bit parts in various school plays and musicals. She graduated from high school the May after that Thanksgiving and enrolled in Wichita State the following September. But, after a year of college, Tracy disappeared. My father tracked her down to Grant Street in Denver where she was living with a married man and his wife. Later the man and Tracy went to California, and we lost contact with them. I became an only child."

When he got to the eighth grade, Nick began to run for his school's track team. Most of the boys wanted to do the sprints, but Nick focused on the distance races. He was competitive, but the real reason he ran was because he simply enjoyed it. The coach told him to back off, that he was running too much. After that, Nick did the long mileage he wanted and needed on Saturdays and Sundays when the coach wasn't around. When he went to college at North Texas State in Denton, just north of Dallas, he ran on an intramural track team and won a few cross-country races.

The classes at North Texas State were not particularly difficult, but, nonetheless, Nick made only so-so grades. His family had expected that he would go to medical school and become a doctor, but he decided that being a doctor was out of reach for him. Anyway, from what he could see, doctors were more like scientists. They had to memorize a bunch of chemistry and biology. He was more interested in working with patients and ministering to their needs. At that time, gender restrictions were being overturned in many American institutions, and across town, Texas Women's University had opened its health sciences program to men. TWU was one of the best nursing schools in Texas, and since Nick liked living in Denton, he decided to continue his studies at TWU and become a nurse.

At his graduation ceremony, Larisa shared her disappointment with him. "You and Tracy have been my whole life. I did everything I could do to help you both succeed. Your father and I have made every sacrifice. Now who knows where Tracy is? Maybe she's dead. Then you decide not to be a doctor. It's that running. If you hadn't wasted so much time running, you could have made better grades. My son is going to be a nurse at the Women's University. What will I tell my friends?"

"But, Mom, being a nurse is what I want to do. And running is what I want to do. I'm sorry, but this is who I am. I wish I could be what you wanted." Nick fought back a tear as he tried to explain himself.

Nick had made the right decision. He excelled at TWU. He had finally found a course of study that excited him. He was eager to get to class and to the hospital each day. He was surrounded by women—Nick was one of the few men in the class—but he didn't date. He was busy, and he felt intimidated by the women, some of whom resented his being there. He didn't think he was gay. The thought of sleeping with another man disgusted him. But he knew his mother wondered if the choice of a career was also a statement about his sexual desires.

Because he did so well at TWU, Nick was offered a job at the Cardiac Center at Methodist Hospital in Houston. He hated leaving Denton and the Dallas area for Houston. Dallas had hills and lakes. Dallas had seasons. Houston was flat, hot, and humid. The Dallas TV stations were always talking about the pollution in Houston. But the Cardiac Center was the premier heart hospital in the world and the chance to work with leading doctors was too attractive to pass up. Nick moved to Houston and continued his running. He became a charter member of the Memorial Park Flyers.

Chapter 7
SHARON

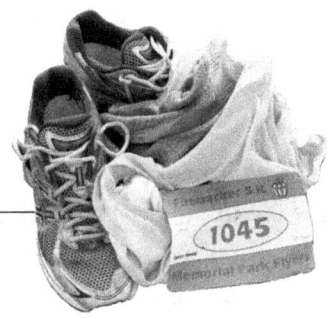

S haron's family had lived in the Philadelphia area since the 1750s. Originally farmers in the fertile lands south and east of the city, they moved into town as the railroads opened up the west and larger farms in Ohio, Illinois, and Indiana replaced the small-scale farming of the Delaware Valley. The founder of the family, John Challner, made a fortune as an early investor in the Pennsylvania Railroad. He used his earnings to buy agricultural properties that lay along the Pennsylvania Main Line, which headed west out of the Philadelphia to Harrisburg. His land became the prime suburban residential developments of Wynnewood, Haverford, and Bryn Mawr.

Sharon's mother and father met at a party after a Princeton football game. Her father, William Adams Challner IV, whom everyone in the family called "Ivy," had bucked family tradition and gone to Princeton instead of the University of Pennsylvania. He thought he would like the rural setting of Princeton and wanted to be his own man. It wasn't exactly an outrageous act of defiance, but Sharon's grandfather and grandmother never quite reconciled themselves to their son's choice of Princeton. Sharon's mother, Lois Bradford Lee, grew up on an estate north of Wilmington, Delaware, on the Brandywine River. She had gone to Barnard College in New York City and was attending the Princeton-Columbia football game with her boyfriend, a student at Columbia.

Ivy and Lois had many friends in common, since the Wilmington and Philadelphia social circles intersected quite often. Ivy was soon trekking to New York to see Lois and enjoy the city's many entertainments. He decided, after all, that he was not suited for country living. There were no good restaurants in Princeton. You could not even find a well-baked loaf of bread there, let alone any decent wine. When Lois and Ivy got married, they settled in Haverford after a brief sojourn to Cambridge so Ivy could attend Harvard Law School. After practicing briefly, he took a position with AT&T, eventually rising to be the company's associate general counsel.

Sharon Challner was born shortly after her parents returned to Haverford. Her brother, Billy, was born a year later. Neither William nor Lois had much time for parenting. William was busy with his work, and Lois was active in charity and cultural groups in Philadelphia. They had a live-in nanny, and both children attended nearby West Chester Friends School. During the summers, Sharon and Billy were sent to Delaware to live with their grandparents, Papa and Mama Lee.

Until she was ten years old, Sharon looked forward to her summers in Delaware. There were picnics and horseback riding. She was somewhat of a tomboy and liked the chores that she did around the estate tagging along behind Papa Lee. By ten, however, she was beginning to go through puberty and develop into the pretty woman she would become. The problem was that her grandfather still liked to play roughhouse. He had always carried her around, and they would pretend to wrestle, rubbing heads together or getting the other one in a bear hug. Now Sharon began to feel uncomfortable around Papa Lee. It seemed he was touching body parts that shouldn't be touched. He pretended that it was an accident, but when his hand slid under her dress, she knew it wasn't an accident.

At first, she mentioned the problem to her nanny, but the nanny said there was nothing she could do and that Sharon should talk to her mother. When her parents came down the next weekend for a visit, Sharon did tell her mother what Papa was doing. Lois brushed it off saying, "That's just the way Papa is. Slap his hand and tell him to stop it." Sharon was afraid to confront her grandfather directly. Maybe she was mistaken and he was just being playful. Maybe he hadn't recognized that she was growing up. She decided to keep quiet and make it through the summer.

The next summer, the summer that Sharon was eleven, her grandmother went to France for a two-week vacation in Cannes. Papa had bought the trip for his wife and her sister. He said it would be a good chance for them to catch up on family things. The first night after Mama Lee left for France, Papa came into Sharon's bedroom in his underwear. It was almost midnight. She could see something sticking out in front of him. He climbed into bed with her, and Sharon could smell whisky on his breath. She told him, "Papa, please don't do this. You shouldn't be here. I'm afraid."

He said, "Hush up. I just want to lie here a little while. You'll see; it will be okay." Sharon tried to get out of the bed, but he held her close to him. She could feel something hard against her leg. After a few minutes he got up to leave.

"Now, Sharon," he said, "this is our little secret. If you tell anybody, then you won't be able to come to the Brandywine any more in the summer."

For the next two weeks, Papa came to Sharon's room every night. Sometimes he would just lie there, and sometimes he would rub his hard thing up and down against her leg. When he was doing the rubbing, he would touch her budding breasts. Sharon would just lie still, softly crying. During the day, she tried to stay away from Papa as much as she could. When Mama Lee came home from France, Sharon told her that she wanted to go back home. She said all her friends were having parties and going riding and she missed them. Papa said no, but Mama Lee understood: "A girl Sharon's age would rather hang around with her friends than be stuck in the country with her old grandparents," she said with a smile. That was the last summer Sharon spent in Delaware.

After that, Papa Lee would try to corner her at family functions and grab her. Most of the time, when he did this, he had been drinking. Sharon learned to stay near her girlfriends whenever he was around. She was now old enough to know what was going on, and she dreaded any contact with her grandfather. She noticed that her mother also avoided Papa and began to wonder if Papa had done the same thing to his daughter when she was younger.

Sharon did not buck family tradition. She went to the University of

Pennsylvania, a private Ivy League college located in downtown Philadelphia. At Penn, Sharon majored in business at the Wharton School,
where she excelled. Sharon's parents, who had supported her through
college, set up a trust fund for her that was quite generous. The only
stipulation in the trust was that Sharon couldn't touch any of the money
until she was thirty years old. They said that they didn't want her blow-
ing her inheritance and figured that, by the time she was thirty, she
would be mature enough to manage her money. She argued with them,
but it was a lost cause.

Freshly out of college, Sharon could live at home if she wanted, but
like most recent college graduates, she considered that her last resort.
Her two options were get a job or get a husband. She had been dating
Jon Muschamp, who was just completing his course work at Penn's law
school. He came from a good Philadelphia family, and they had known
each other since they were at the Friends School. Sharon remembered
everyone at Friends making fun of his first name, which he insisted be
pronounced "yawn." The "ch" in his last name was to be soft. Thus he
was called "yawn moo-shamp."

Jon was going to work for the U.S. attorney in Houston, Texas, after
he passed his bar exam. In the months surrounding graduations, people
seem particularly susceptible to getting married. It is a time of transition, when many aspects of your life are in flux. Sharon had finished
her undergraduate degree and had no idea what she wanted to do with
herself. Jon was heading off to—God forbid—Texas. They decided that
they would make a good couple. Both sets of parents agreed.

Wealthy society types don't often get married on the spur of the moment. It takes a year to make the arrangements and to get onto people's
calendars. It was decided that Jon would go ahead to Houston and the
wedding would take place in Philadelphia the following April. That was
a tight schedule, but Lois thought she could manage it. Jon made several trips home, and Sharon traveled to Houston to help pick out a
house. The wedding was a big success. After their honeymoon in Maine,
Sharon joined Jon in their small bungalow in West University, a village
located next to Rice University and now totally surrounded by the City
of Houston.

Sharon realized almost immediately that marrying Jon was a mistake. He was angry about life. He didn't want to be a lawyer, he didn't want to be a prosecutor, and he didn't want to live in Texas. All these things were part of his father's plan to get him into national politics. Jon wanted a quiet, comfortable life as a businessman. He could fill up his days managing his inheritance and make more than enough money to live comfortably. To ease his anger, Jon drank. Usually he started before he got home. When Jon was drunk, he became a hitter. In his mind, Sharon was a co-conspirator, pushing him into a life he hadn't chosen. She was the only one near enough to hit, so he hit her. As had been the case with her grandfather, Sharon had to carefully manage her husband.

On the other hand, Sharon found that she loved Houston. She liked being away from her family and the whole Philadelphia social scene. For the first time in her life, she felt she was her own woman. She liked the hot weather and the outdoor lifestyle in Houston. She definitely did not miss the snowy, cold East Coast winters. She quickly made friends in her new neighborhood, and they invited her into their social network. She joined the Junior League and was appointed to the board of the Memorial Park Conservancy. She had found her home.

Sharon's friends began to notice black and blue marks on her arms and the occasional black eye. When she showed up for a board meeting with a broken arm, Sharon told everyone she had tripped on a rug. Before long, it was impossible to hide what was going on. With encouragement from her support group, Sharon filed for divorce after fourteen months of marriage.

Jon wasn't surprised, and he didn't contest the divorce. He was relieved to be out of a relationship he never really wanted. Texas doesn't have alimony, and anyway, the couple had a prenuptial agreement that protected both Jon's and Sharon's family funds. Sharon's lawyer maintained that because of the violence in the marriage and the fact that Jon worked for the United States attorney's office, Jon should come up with some funds for Sharon to live on. It could prove embarrassing if the truth were publicly known.

Jon agreed to pay Sharon an allowance of $7,000 per month for six years. By that time, Sharon would be thirty years old and could tap her trust fund if she needed money for living expenses. Sharon also got the house, which she quickly sold for quite a bit more than was owed on the mortgage. Sharon rented a nice townhouse on the border of River Oaks, the wealthiest section of Houston. She was set financially.

Sharon told me that this was probably the happiest time of her life. "I was free in a new city with plenty of money and plenty of friends. I immersed myself in charitable activities. I dated around with guys my age up to guys my dad's age. None of it was serious until I met Skip."

Skip Fleming was two years older than Sharon and well connected in Houston society. He was an oil and gas wheeler and dealer and projected an image that reminded her of J.R. Ewing on the hit TV show *Dallas*. He certainly walked the walk and talked the talk. Besides, Skip was a lot more fun than the other men she had been dating. He liked to party.

After they had been seeing each other for a couple of months, Skip suggested that he move in with her. Sharon didn't think that was a good idea. She didn't know him that well and still wasn't sure if Skip was the right man for her or if she would ever marry again. She certainly did not want to get into a de facto marriage. Then, a year later, out of the blue, Skip asked her to marry him. They had met for dinner at Damien's, an upscale Italian restaurant near downtown. It was one of Sharon's favorites. Just before dinner, Skip pulled a ring out of his pocket and asked her to marry him. Surprising herself, Sharon accepted, and they spent the night at her place. The next day Skip moved into Sharon's townhouse. They were married in Hawaii a few months later. Only close friends were invited.

Soon after they were married, Skip's oil company began to fall apart. Sharon didn't know exactly what was going on, but she knew it wasn't good. Skip didn't like to talk about it. After his company closed down, Skip spent most days in front of the TV. Since her husband had never been one for TV, Sharon believed he was just using it as a pacifier to avoid confronting his problems. Maybe he needed some feel good pills to bring him out of his gloom.

When Skip's father passed away, he once again had funds of his own and built a new house in West University on one of the larger lots. It was not like the country houses that Sharon had grown up in on the

Main Line, but it was comfortable and large enough to entertain their many friends. The house project and the managing of his father's estate seemed to break Skip out of his depression. He became more active and got involved with some new business projects. It had been a rough way to start a marriage, but they were through that trial now. With two kids, a renewed husband, and a new house, Sharon was happy.

Skip was now over forty, and he decided he needed to do something to stave off old age. He was still in good shape by most standards, but he had put on a few pounds during the crisis years. Sharon had heard about the Memorial Park Flyers running club while working on the board of the Memorial Park Conservancy. Both Sharon and Skip decided that running a marathon would be a good way to lose a few pounds. The following July they joined the Flyers.

Skip was not really interested in running. He was doing it for health and glamour reasons. Sharon, however, found a new passion. "I loved getting outside, running through the neighborhoods surrounding the park," she said. "I met some women my age, and we quickly became best friends. My other activities had been a matter of duty, but running was a matter of love. It was my new religion."

Sharon had not really known much about the Flyers when she started running with them. She assumed it was a club, but she soon noticed that Kurt Harding, the head coach, ran it like his own company. He was somewhat obnoxious and often tried to flirt with her in a way she didn't appreciate. He liked to put his arm around her shoulders after a run and pull her too close, putting his face just inches from hers to talk. He also had created a cadre of assistant coaches who seemed to be adopting his mannerisms. She loved the other runners but didn't like the leadership.

Sharon decided to check into the legal status of the Flyers. What she found convinced her that Kurt was not operating the club in line with the IRS requirements for a charitable organization. When Kurt made Bill Smithers, one of his more abusive henchmen, head coach, Sharon decided it was time to act. She organized a protest that came to a head at a coach's training session before the start of the new season. The meeting quickly got out of hand as insults were exchanged between Sharon's supporters and Kurt's supporters. I suggested that we assemble a smaller group at my office in a couple of days and offered to act as a mediator. Sharon and Kurt agreed to meet. I told them, "Bring your lawyers and no more than two other people. Be prepared to make a brief presentation on what you want to achieve."

At my office, the atmosphere was tense and acrimonious. In my experience, that is often the case in mediations. The mediator is there because the two sides are too mad to talk directly to each other. I asked Sharon to speak first. "My group wants to establish a set of bylaws and elect officers to run the Flyers," she said. "If that doesn't happen, we're prepared to pursue legal action against Kurt and the Flyers on a number of fronts including sexual harassment."

When Kurt got his turn to speak, he said, "I own the Flyers, and I am free to choose whomever I want to coach in the program. I admit that there have been some issues with the IRS, but my attorneys and accountants are resolving those problems." Kurt flatly denied that he had engaged in sexual harassment and said, "If any of my coaches are guilty of offensive conduct, they will be out immediately. All you have to do is let me know." It was clear that Kurt's lawyer had coached him thoroughly. Frankly, it was an impressive show.

As mediator, it was not my job to decide who was right and who was wrong. I was not an arbitrator. My job was to get the parties to resolve the dispute themselves. To do that, I spoke with each side in private. I first met with Sharon and her contingent. Carol, another runner with the Flyers, was acting as Sharon's attorney. "As far as I can see," I said, "all you can do is cause Kurt a lot of trouble and perhaps kill the Flyers. While you make some good points about Kurt's personal conduct and his management of the Flyers, none of those points are likely to lead to you gaining control of the club."

Then Sharon dropped her bomb. "I have talked to the mayor's office, and if I want to start another running club, I can have exclusive use Memorial Park for Saturday runs. I would much prefer to turn the Flyers into a real club, but if I am forced to, I will start a new club and put Kurt out of business. I don't want to threaten him directly, but he has to go along with what we want." Sharon and her friends were prepared to play hardball.

I then met with Kurt and his team. He had brought Matt Dingle, his corporate lawyer, with him. Matt was not a runner, but he knew a lot about the business side of the Flyers operation. I told Kurt, "I agree with a lot of the points you made in your opening statement, but you are missing the forest for the trees. The real issue is a business one, not a legal one. Sharon and the assistant coaches have essentially taken over the Flyers at the grass-roots level. You can fight them and probably win a legal victory, but it would be meaningless. The Flyers would be dead." Without telling him that Sharon had already talked to the mayor's office about the use of Memorial Park, I suggested that if Sharon decided to set up a competing club, the Flyers would likely fold.

Kurt slumped in his chair. "Fine," he said, "I'd like it if they all just went away and left me alone. They never understood what running was about anyway."

Luckily, Matt could see immediately the position his client was in. Matt was accustomed to negotiating business deals, and it was obvious to him who had the power here. He asked, "What exactly will it take for Sharon to back off with the IRS and drop the harassment charges? I still can't tell what they actually want out of this deal." I could tell that Matt might actually help me resolve this impasse.

Back in the other room, Carol said their bottom line was simple: "A standard set of bylaws should be put in place for the Flyers, and an election should be held to choose officers. All members would be allowed to vote." She added, as an afterthought, "Kurt should agree not to stand for election for any office. I expect that he would be voted out, but I don't want him to run and complicate the process."

While I had been with Sharon's group, Matt had been working on Kurt trying to get him to see the reality of his situation, which was not good. I told Kurt what Sharon's bottom line was. He admitted that even if he ran for office, he would probably lose. They were basically asking him to give up the Flyers.

"Has anyone said anything about the Flyers Firecracker 5K? You know the Fourth of July race," Matt asked.

"No, that has not been mentioned." I was totally focused on the club and had completely forgotten about the race. I knew it had been a successful event and was likely to grow in the future.

Matt laid out a possible path of compromise. Sharon would get her bylaws. In fact, she was free to put in them whatever she liked. Kurt would maintain control and ownership of the Firecracker 5k, but in the future, there would be no connection between the Flyers and the race. In return, Sharon's group would desist from interfering with Kurt's dealings with the IRS and would drop the sexual harassment lawsuits.

Kurt didn't like the proposal. "I worked hard to make the Flyers a success," he said. "They're pulling the rug out from under me. For Sharon this is just a rich girl's lark. She's got nothing better to do with herself. For me, well, for me, this is my sweat and blood. I'd rather have nothing than agree to this joke of a settlement. They can all go to hell!" It was clear to me that Kurt's emotions were getting in the way of his reason. I asked Matt to come to my office to meet with Carol. I thought that with just the lawyers we might get a settlement.

In my office Carol immediately pointed out, "There is no way that I or anyone else can ensure that the three women who have come forward will not file harassment charges against Kurt. I think they are unlikely to do so if Kurt is out of the Flyers, but we can't guarantee it. I like the idea of splitting the race and the club apart. None of my people really care about the race one way or another."

Matt then spoke, "We need to give Kurt a face-saving option or he is likely to take the whole thing down. I have known him a long time, and he can be pretty hard headed. Requiring Kurt to commit in writing not to stand for election is just rubbing his nose in it for no purpose. Kurt already told me that he expected to lose any election in which all the members were allowed to vote."

"I agree that Kurt's bowing out of the election can be left as a side verbal understanding. I doubt he would want the embarrassment of being voted out of office," Carol said.

"Good, we agree on that. Kurt owns this club, and you all are going to have to pay him something to get it. How about if Kurt is appointed 'Head Coach Emeritus', and the club retains him as a consultant for four years with an annual retainer of $25,000? That will give him some money, and with that, I think he will agree to step aside."

Carol replied, "I don't like the idea of him having any association with the Flyers at all. As to the amount of money, we will have to talk about it. I'm not against him getting something out of the deal."

We called everyone together again, and I explained what was going to happen. I outlined the proposed settlement and told them we would not discuss it any further until Matt and Carol had prepared the necessary documents. I warned, "Neither side will totally like the outcome, but that is why it is called a compromise. I think this is a reasonable way to go forward. Litigation or continued squabbling would likely kill the Flyers, and I don't think any of us want that."

Two weeks later, the settlement was agreed to by both parties. Kurt was retained as a "Consulting Coach" for two years at fee of $15,000 per year. Subsequently, Sharon was elected president, and Carol was elected treasurer. Kurt did not run for an office.

Chapter 8
SKIP

S kip Fleming and his wife Sharon joined the Flyers the year after I did. He ran about the same pace as I did, and we did many Saturday runs together. He was without a doubt one of the nicest and smartest guys I have ever met. He was born Robert Lewis Fleming III on Galveston Island in 1949. Few people live in Galveston, and even fewer are born there. Those that are form a tight-knit brotherhood know as BOI (Born On the Island). Skip's grandfather, Robert Lewis Fleming, came to Galveston to work as a stevedore in 1898. He survived the hurricane of 1900 and went into the construction business helping to rebuild the devastated city. He eventually got into the tourism industry and owned a hotel and nightclub where bootleg booze, gambling, and sex were openly available. At that time, Galveston was vying with New Orleans and Havana for the title of best sin city in the Western Hemisphere. Las Vegas was still a desert outpost.

Skip's father, known as Bob, was a quiet, studious boy who developed an interest in medicine at an early age. The University of Texas Medical Branch is located in Galveston. Established in 1891, UTMB was the first medical school in Texas. Bob liked to walk over to the medical library in his spare time. Because of the notoriety of his father, the doctors knew Bob and invited him to attend seminars or observe operations when he was old enough. Bob went to Rice and then came back to Galveston for medical school. When Skip was growing up, Dr. Bob, as everyone in Galveston called him, was chief of surgery and on the board of UTMB's John Sealy Hospital.

Skip was somewhere between his grandfather and his father in terms of personality and temperament. He was smart, but his interests were never focused. The one thing he took seriously was sailing. His grandfather had a forty-two-foot sailboat, which was considered a large boat at that time. Skip spent his spare time at the marina talking to sailors and learning everything he could about sailing. He loved to go out on the boat, and once a year, he and his grandfather would take a cruise to Mexico or some other exotic place. When he was eight years old, his grandfather gave him a cap for Christmas that said "Robert Fleming, Skipper" on it. After that, everyone called him "Skip."

Skip went to Southern Methodist University in Dallas. He joined the Sigma Alpha Epsilon fraternity and spent much of his time working on SAE parties. Whenever asked, he said he was majoring in beer and broads. Luckily for him, Skip was smart enough to make gentlemen's Bs with very little work. Part of his problem was that he didn't like Dallas. It was an inland city with a distinct Texas ranching flavor to it. Even though he was wealthy, he found the Dallas social scene snooty and pretentious. He liked the wide open lifestyles of Houston, Los Angeles, and Miami. He got out of town on the weekends whenever his fraternity wasn't staging a big social event.

Somewhere along the way Skip decided that it would be a good idea to get a law degree. He didn't have a lot of interest in being a lawyer, but it would give him three more years in school and he was sure he could do well without much work. To his surprise, the University of Texas School of Law rejected his application. It was his first indication that family connections and wealth might not be enough to open every door for him. UT Law was the best law school in Texas and one of the best in the country. Skip asked his father if he could help him get into UT, and Dr. Bob agreed to call Governor John Connally. Dr. Bob and Connally had served on several boards together, and Connally was interested in running for national office in the future. Like any successful politician, he was anxious to court people with money and agreed to meet with Skip.

Skip drove to Austin and met with the governor in his executive office at the capitol building. Governor Connally asked Skip about his time at SMU and about his plans for the future. He then told Skip that he could call his good friend Frank Erwin, who was chairman of the UT Board of Regents, and ask him to admit Skip to the law school. But then, he said, everyone would eventually find out how Skip had gotten in and that would not be a good situation. Connally advised Skip to, instead, look at the excellent law schools in Houston, specifically the University of Houston.

What the governor didn't know was that the U of H Law School was also hard to get into, but Dr. Bob had more immediate contacts there and got involved from the beginning. Skip was admitted and, for the first time in his life, decided to concentrate on his studies. He did well in his classes and was named to the *Law Review*. In spite of his success, he still didn't really want to be a lawyer. Several of the big Houston firms offered him a job, but he didn't like the idea of working the hours that associate attorneys put in.

Instead of practicing law, he decided to get into oil and gas. The Arab Oil Embargo had dramatically increased the price of crude, and Houston was booming. Two of his SAE fraternity brothers had started SigEx, an oil and gas exploration and production company. They invited Skip to join them as an equity partner. They knew Skip's family had a lot of money and that he was well connected in the wealthier parts of Texas society. One of Skip's partners, Alex Gomez, was from Laredo and on a trip home had noticed that the Mexicans were drilling gas wells just across the Rio Grande. Although Alex was not a geologist, he figured that the gas fields didn't stop at the river. He began buying up mineral leases, but he needed money to drill and develop the properties. Skip was supposed to supply the funds.

To rub elbows with Houston's movers and shakers, Skip joined the River Oaks Country Club and began attending charity galas. The women in Houston enjoyed putting on fancy balls but felt guilty about it if they didn't involve a charity. The standard format was to rent a country club for the night, bring in a good dance band, and auction off donated items that ranged from a meal for two at a local watering hole to a trip to Switzerland. At one, a live pot-bellied pig went unsold after the frightened animal relieved itself on the matron holding him. A popular item was a ride for six in the Goodyear blimp. That usually went for several thousand dollars. It was at one of these galas that Skip met Sharon.

Skip did his homework, and when he found out about Sharon's background, he immediately thought that the Challner family might want to invest in his company. They were the ideal target: rich Yankees. Skip asked Sharon out and began to court her, or at least her money. Eventually, they became an item and appeared in the local gossip rags that reported on the comings and goings of high society. They made one trip to Philadelphia to meet Sharon's family, but, if anyone asked, they were still "just friends."

Like everyone in the oil patch in the late 1970s, Skip's only problem was carrying money to the bank. In 1981, crude was near $40 a barrel, and forecasters predicted that it would go to $100. The smart money was buying up property and pouring money into drilling. Then in 1982, the price collapsed and the boom was over. Skip's company had leveraged its equity as much as it could. SigEx had never made much money, but funds flowing in from new investors covered interest payments and allowed the company to keep pushing forward.

There is a fine line between the oil business at this level and a run-of-the-mill Ponzi scheme. When the price of oil turned down, the spigot of cash flowing in from new investors went dry. Suddenly, cash from operations was needed to service the debt, but the company was already fully committed to capital expenditures. Skip and his partners were desperate. Skip admitted to me later that he liked Sharon, but his decision to marry her had been based on the hope that he could use some of her money to get through the cash flow crisis.

Skip arranged to have dinner at Damien's, Sharon's favorite Italian restaurant. They had gone there on their first real date, and he thought that it would be the perfect place to ask Sharon to marry him.

At Damien's, Skip ordered a bottle of champagne and just before dinner arrived said, "Sharon, I have given this a lot of thought, and I'm sure you're the woman I have been waiting for all this time." At that point, he got down on one knee beside the table "I love you. Will you marry me?" He pulled his grandmother's engagement ring out of his pocket and offered it to her.

Sharon had a feeling that Skip might ask her to marry him, and she had also given it quite a bit of thought. She wanted children, and she wasn't the type to have a child out of wedlock. She enjoyed Skip's company, and he didn't seem to mind the various clubs and activities that took so much of her time. She had become adept at managing men. She had had to. She felt that Skip was someone she could manage.

No one else was waiting in the wings, and her biological clock was ticking. Still, she was unsure of what she wanted to do. Then he asked her to marry him in the middle of Damien's, and she found herself saying, "Yes, yes, yes. Just get up. People are staring at us." Skip stood up and gave her a quick kiss. She slipped the ring on. It fit perfectly.

Sharon's mother, Lois, wanted to put on a wedding in Houston, but Sharon and Skip opted for a destination wedding in Hawaii. When they returned from their honeymoon, Lois threw a fancy party for them at the Junior League.

The oil and gas market went south so fast that Skip had no time to tap the resources of his new in-laws. He found out later that the Challner family believed that there were only two important things in life: family and money. If there were ever a conflict between those two, then there was only money. This principle had served them well for two hundred years. He would not likely have gotten much help from them.

SigEx went into receivership, and its assets were sold off by the bankruptcy trustee. Skip had lost his investment and so had all the other investors. Of course, many other companies were also going under. The oilman's prayer at the time was, "Lord, give me one more boom. I promise not to piss it away this time." Still Skip felt guilty about losing his friends' money. No one really blamed him, but he blamed himself. For a while he did nothing. The couple lived on Sharon's money.

Then, when his father died in 1987, Skip managed the probate process and began to take an interest in investing his newfound wealth. He was determined to stay conservative in his investments this time and not blow everything he had. Between his income and Sharon's income, they were wealthy but not super-rich by Houston standards. Neither of them needed to worry about earning a living.

By the early 1990s, Skip had developed an interest in the recording industry. "Austin was a little Nashville, and there were plenty of musicians in Texas who were looking for a backer to help get that first record out," Skip told me during one of our runs. "I knew that this was not a way to make money. In fact, it was a good way to lose money, but I thought so long as I limited my investments, it would make a reasonable hobby."

Skip got to meet some interesting people and to bum around Nashville, LA, and New York with the entertainment crowd. A few of his artists were actually successful in the Texas folk market made popular by Willie Nelson and Waylon Jennings.

By the time I met Skip and Sharon, they were twelve years into their marriage. Skip had grown concerned with his physical appearance. In the record business, he was mostly around younger performers, and he was beginning to feel old. He suggested that they start running, and Sharon told him about the Flyers. They signed up that summer. Neither of them was a disaster in terms of their weight. Skip had gained twenty pounds since college but still looked trim. Sharon would be considered thin by most people's standards.

The spring after they completed their first Houston Marathon, Sharon disappeared to California for a few weeks, or at least I didn't see her for a while. When she came back, the skin on her face was stretched tightly across her cheekbones. It was clear that she had had a face lift. A similar disappearance in May resulted in a new, or enhanced, set of breasts. Sharon had been on the skinny side, and her bustline had been proportional to the rest of her body. Now she was a little top heavy, not grotesquely so, but enough that it didn't look quite natural.

Skip coached the back of the pack, 5/1 walk-run group. The 5/1 people ran for five minutes and walked for one minute. This allowed their heart rates to recover and for them to have an easier, and usually faster, time in the marathon. Many of these slower runners were young women whom Skip loved to regale with his stories about various stars he had met. He often serenaded them with pop songs, and sometimes they would join in. It was quite a sight to see them coming in from a run. He looked like the Pied Piper leading the children of Hamlin.

At the start of each season, Skip would walk me around the meeting area pointing out the new meat. He was both funny and scathing in his evaluation of the female runners. He would try to recruit the best-looking ones for his group. This year, he was especially hot on a twenty-something girl named Jessica. She was a well-tanned, white girl with a beautiful face and a perfect body. Skip began hanging around with her before, during, and after the runs. Jessica liked Skip's attention because he was popular, because he was a coach, and, probably, because he was married. Many young women don't mind flirting with older married guys precisely because they think they are harmless.

Skip's infatuation with Jess, as he liked to call her, became obvious to me at a party Sharon threw for her supporters to celebrate her election as president of the club. There were over a hundred people at their house in West U. Runners like to drink and party. One of the reasons for running is to allow the ingestion of excessive amounts of food and alcohol.

The only problem with the Flemings' home for entertaining was that there was only one bathroom on the first floor. When they were having a big party, it was often necessary to go to the second floor powder room. On one trek upstairs, I happened to notice Skip and Jessica, heading into the master bedroom. I thought maybe he was going to show her some of the posters of his recording stars. He had already shown these to me earlier that evening, but then the door closed and I heard the lock click.

Later, I asked him, "Skip, what were you and Jessica doing behind locked doors?"

Skip quickly replied, "Man, I can't get away with anything. The truth is Jess wanted to see some of my recording junk, and I didn't want everybody coming in there."

"Right. What's wrong? Doesn't Sharon take care of you anymore, bud?" I asked.

"Oh sure, she pretty much will suck me off any time I ask her to. And we get it on every now and then, especially if we've had a little weed."

"What's the problem then? Why are you messing around with another girl?"

Skip paused before replying, "I don't really know. I look at Sharon and see a wonderful woman. She is still pretty and treats me good. We have a great house and all that. But I guess she just doesn't do it for me anymore. It is hard to explain. When I am with Jess, I just feel good. It's kind of like the feeling I get after a really hard ten-mile run. I am relaxed. I feel at peace with the world."

It was soon clear to everyone that Skip was hitting on Jessica. Guys that are truly "in love" don't do a good job of hiding it. When discussing the actions of a buck during rut, the Texas Wildlife Department put it this way, "Buck deer, like most male mammals, seem to lose a lot of their natural caution when the scent of a receptive female is in the air."

I am sure that Sharon noticed Skip's behavior because, suddenly, she made a quick trip to California. When she returned, her faced looked like she had gotten extremely sunburned. Sharon told me that she had had a chemical dermal abrasion. It was supposed to remove the old skin on the surface of her face so that the new, younger skin would be exposed. I asked her, "Why in the world would you do such a thing? You're already the prettiest girl in the Flyers!"

Her response was, "Skip likes younger looking women."

I couldn't very well tell her what Skip had confided in me. You can lose weight, you can tone up, you can learn a new trick, but you can't take the years off. I suspect Sharon was well into menopause and her body was just no longer producing the chemical signals needed to turn Skip on. It wasn't a matter of looks or style. It was a matter of juice. She just couldn't juice him anymore.

A University of New Mexico professor found that strippers earned twice as much in tips while they were ovulating than they did otherwise. As the Texas Wildlife Department pointed out, males respond to females in heat. When a woman quits ovulating, she can have a problem with her husband. It is not exactly front page news that many a man has left his wife for a younger woman, unless, of course, it's the president or a senator. Then the press acts shocked and trumpets the scandal for as long as it sells papers. Can anyone truly believe that this is unusual behavior or that it is voluntary?

It wasn't long after her abrasion that Sharon called me. I rarely spoke to the women in my club, except at runs or at parties. E-mail was my preferred method of communication, so I was definitely surprised when I answered the phone and heard Sharon's voice. She said, "Skip and I are going to counseling. Well, actually, it is a mediator."

This sounded fishy to me so I asked, "Like what issues are you discussing?"

She said, "We might be getting divorced. We both want it to be friendly, so we are trying to work through who will get what or even if we want to do it."

Now I knew it was fishy. "And just how did this mediation come about?" I asked.

"Skip's lawyer knew this fellow and thought he could help us," she told me.

"And what did your lawyer think?" was my next question.

"Oh, I don't have a lawyer. I want this to be friendly," she said.

"Sharon, the best way to make this friendly is for both of you to have lawyers. That way you can be the friendliest person in the great state of Texas and let your lawyer do the dirty work. I will e-mail you the name of a couple of the best divorce attorneys in Houston." My brother had gone through a nasty divorce a few years earlier, so I knew who she should call. I asked, "Will you promise to call one of these guys?"

"I promise," she said with some reluctance in her voice. I could tell that she wanted to be friends with Skip, even if they were no longer going to be married.

Chapter 9

CANDY

D ulce Romero is a first generation American. Her father came to the United States from Saltillo, Mexico. He entered this country without papers, but later married a U.S. citizen and eventually became a citizen himself. Dulce grew up on the east side of town near the Houston Ship Channel where the Mexican populace keeps well-maintained houses surrounded by yards decorated in traditional Mexican colors of bright greens, reds, and yellows. She met her husband Rogelio at the old San Jacinto High School. Now converted to administrative offices, it was named in honor of the battle in which General Sam Houston defeated General Santa Anna to win the independence of Texas from Mexico. Ironically, when Dulce and Rogelio went there, almost all the students in the school were Hispanic.

Dulce and Rogelio fell in love and vowed to make it in this Anglo-dominated city. The first step was to anglicize their names to Candy and Roger. Then they developed a financial game plan. Candy would sell automobile insurance, while Roger worked construction. At nights and on the weekends, they started a carpet installation business. It meant long hours for both of them, but they were committed to making it work.

Soon the carpet business was going well enough that Roger could quit his construction job. Candy continued to work at the insurance agency so they could have medical benefits. They had three children, two boys and one girl, and were able to move to a larger house in Katy, a suburb on the west side of Houston. By the time the youngest boy was in high school, it looked like they had it made. Candy and Roger started thinking about buying some property in Mexico close to her father's family for a retirement home.

Candy joined the Memorial Park Flyers after Roger got sick. He had been feeling weak for several months but was too busy with work to go to a doctor. Like most men, he didn't really like hanging around doctors' offices or hospitals. When he finally went in for a checkup, his doctor wanted to do a bunch of tests and Roger put them off as long as he could. When the results came back, they weren't good. He had liver problems. A biopsy confirmed the MRI: Roger had cancer.

Liver cancer varies widely in its severity and the outlook for the patient. Roger's doctor thought his cancer might respond to chemotherapy and started him immediately on an aggressive treatment. Candy started running just to calm her fears and relieve the tension. There was nothing anyone could do but wait and pray. Candy and Roger were Catholics who believed strongly in the power of prayer. Candy put more trust in God than she did in the doctors.

Roger's condition went unchanged for several months. Chemo is hard on the body, and he was weak. He couldn't do anything strenuous but still went out with his installation crews to make sure they were doing a good job for his customers. When I met Roger at a party, he looked healthy to me except for the black and blue spots on his arms where multiple IVs had been implanted. Since I had just met him, I couldn't say for sure, but it appeared he was wearing a wig. We talked; he seemed okay. It surprises me that the human body can be very sick and still function normally. It is a short slippery slope between being alive and being dead.

Just after Christmas, Roger's condition took a dramatic turn for the worse. Several of the Flyers suggested that we should hold a prayer meeting for Roger. About twenty of us gathered at Carol's home. Loretta had agreed to lead the service. Her father was a minister in a Pentecostal church near Dallas. Since she had been exposed to church all her life, she knew how to lead a prayer meeting. The group consisted of people from just about every Christian tradition, but we all were comfortable in our ecumenicalism.

Loretta asked us to join hands and led us in an opening prayer, "Dear Heavenly Father, we gather here this evening to beseech you to hear our prayers for the restoration of the health of your faithful servant, Roger. We pray that You grant him the health that only You can give. Comfort his wife Candy and their children. Show us the way to live our lives so that Thy will be done. We ask these things in the name of Thy Holy Son, Jesus Christ. Amen."

We then had few minutes of silence as we kept our heads bowed and hands clasped. A hand squeeze marked the end of the prayer, and Loretta again said, "Amen." Sharon then read a poem that she had written for Roger and Candy. The title of the poem was "Rejoice!"

We want to know the future.
Turn to the back of the book,
See how it ends.

No better at foretelling the future
Than ancients cutting open chickens,
We put our faith in labs and machinery.

In a marathon we all know
Exactly where comes the finish,
But must take one step at a time.

You cannot know this finish.
Keep your faith in the one, true, and living God.
Rejoice in the journey that will be provided. Amen.

The reading brought tears to Candy's eyes. After a few minutes of quiet discussion, Carol played the Beatles song "Let It Be!" on her stereo. The first few lines seemed especially relevant: "When I find myself in times of trouble, Mother Mary comes to me, speaking words of wisdom, let it be, let it be." The song is based on the biblical story of the visit of Archangel Gabriel to Mary telling her that she is to be the mother of God. She asks, "Why me?" But Mary then relents and accepts God's will saying, in effect, "Let it be!"

Loretta next led us in the reading of Twenty-third Psalm:

The Lord is my Shepherd; I shall not want.
He maketh me to lie down in green pastures:
He leadeth me beside the still waters.
He restoreth my soul:
He leadeth me in the paths of righteousness for His name's sake.

Yea, though I walk through the valley of the shadow of death,
I will fear no evil:
For thou art with me;
Thy rod and thy staff, they comfort me.
Thou preparest a table before me in the presence of mine
*   enemies;*
Thou annointest my head with oil;
My cup runneth over.
Surely goodness and mercy shall follow me all the days of my life,
*   and I will dwell in the House of the Lord forever.*

Doyle, who is an assistant pastor at his church, led us all in an a cappella singing of "The Old Rugged Cross." He had brought copies of the lyrics, and everyone seemed familiar with the tune. After the song, each of us gave Candy a hug and spoke a few private words to her. We joined hands once more and concluded the service with the saying of the "Lord's Prayer." At the end of the prayer, there was a spontaneous group hug in which we surrounded Candy and came together into a tight ball.

Roger seemed to be improving for a few weeks, but then Candy sent out an e-mail telling us that he had been moved to a hospice. Hospice care is a relatively new medical service for those whom the doctors can no longer help. You go there to die. The treatment at a hospice focuses on easing the death process and relieving pain rather than prolonging life. Candy and her children sat with Roger at all times. Runners and members of Candy's church dropped by to visit. I went there twice.

The hospice was quiet and soothing. It was not at all like a busy hospital ward. Roger lay comatose on the bed. He had an IV hooked up to his left arm. His breathing was quiet, showing no strain. After a week, the family made the difficult decision to discontinue all life support and commend Roger's fate to Jesus. He held on for five more days and then peacefully passed away.

I have never been a believer in a physical, personal God that answers individual prayers. It made me a little uncomfortable to be around so many people who felt a close connection to a God in Heaven who listened to their petitions. I have a scientific background and look to science for explanations of events. My experience with these "true believers" made me reconsider my own philosophical, and scientific, position. I could see that the prayers, especially the group prayers, were comforting to Candy.

From running I know that it is possible for the body itself to produce narcotics which act like heroin on the brain. Heroin and other opiates work precisely because the brain has receptors for this class of chemicals. Around mile twenty-three in a marathon, I usually am swamped with emotion and often begin to cry. It is not something I am consciously or intellectually responding to. It is my body trying to deal with the pain by manufacturing drugs that I can't legally buy without a prescription.

Religions have developed techniques to induce the production of these same chemicals. Buddhists meditate, Dervishes whirl, priests lead elaborate rituals, and preachers pound the Bible. All these are designed to produce an internal chemical response that is comforting to the participants. On Christmas Eve, as I watch the candle-lit procession with golden crosses leading the robed celebrants to the altar and listen to the choir singing "O Come, All Ye Faithful," I experience a feeling not dissimilar to that at the end of a marathon. In our own amateur way, we were using these time-tested religious rituals to comfort Candy and ourselves.

I am somewhat amused by Stephen Hawking and other physicists who dismiss religions because their simple, traditional myths are not consistent with current cosmology. Those nonbelievers miss the spiritual aspect of worship and its very real scientific basis in the chemistry of the brain. Even medical doctors are now recognizing that belief in the efficacy of a sugar pill can ease pain because the body responds to that belief by releasing soothing drugs. There are many paths but only one way.

Luckily, Candy had her children, her church, her job, and her running. She sold their carpet business to one of the senior employees. She grieved for a while but then moved on. At age fifty, she still had a life to live and no time to waste. The women of the club rallied around her. She became close friends with Sally, who was also single. She began to focus on her finishing times and became one of our faster runners. She won her age division in a few local races.

Candy even started to date again. She told me that she and Roger had had a successful marriage. "While I greatly miss my Roger and know no man can replace him, I don't want to go into old age alone," she said. She met Ken, also a runner, at her church. Ken had just moved to Houston, and Candy enjoyed showing him around the city and introducing him to her friends. Ken was thinking about joining the Flyers and one Saturday showed up at breakfast after our long run. I liked the guy immediately. He was somewhat soft spoken but had interesting things to say. He definitely liked Candy. I could tell that she appreciated the attention he lavished on her. I expected to see a lot more of him in the future.

That afternoon I received an e-mail from Candy with the subject line reading "Prayer Request!" That is never good news. When Candy had gotten home from breakfast, she found a message from the wife of her older son, Rogelio. Rogelio was named after his father but had decided to keep the Spanish name to avoid being called Junior and because it was now cool to be Hispanic. Rogelio had gotten married ten months ago and was in medical school in Cincinnati. His wife told Candy that Rogelio had not been feeling well and had checked himself into the hospital where he worked. It turned out that he had multiple severe infections and immediately had been put into ICU isolation, sedated, and started on a regimen of broad spectrum antibiotics. She told Candy to come as quickly as possible.

When the culprit was finally identified by the lab, it turned out that Rogelio was suffering from an MRSA staph infection. MRSA stands for methicillin-resistant Staphylococcus aureus. It is a bug resistant to most drugs and can kill within a few hours. Had Rogelio waited another hour, he probably would never have made it to the hospital. Even at this point, the outlook was bleak. His lungs were severely compromised, and he was on 100 percent ventilation. The doctors gave Rogelio less than a 50 percent chance of survival. From my quick research on the Internet, it sounded to me like they were being overly optimistic. Few people live once the infection has reached this stage.

Candy immediately flew to Cincinnati. It turned out that a fellow Flyer who had moved there last year lived only four blocks from the hospital where Rogelio was being treated. She invited Candy to stay with her since Rogelio's apartment was on the other side of town. When Candy saw Rogelio, it was déjà vu. There was her son totally sedated, hooked up to tubes, electric monitors, and a breathing apparatus. Only now she could not go into the room where he was for fear that she would be contaminated or that she would contaminate him. How could this be happening to her again when she was getting her life back together after losing Roger? A priest prayed with her in the hospital chapel.

In Houston the prayers were flowing back and forth over the Internet between members of our breakfast group. Loretta, in recognition that both Candy and her family were devout Catholics, found a prayer to Mary:

Remember, O most gracious Virgin Mary,
that never was it known
that anyone who fled to thy protection,
implored thy help
or sought thy intercession,
was left unaided.

Inspired by this confidence,
We fly unto thee, O Virgin of virgins my Mother;
to thee do we come, before thee we stand, sinful and sorrowful;
O Mother of the Word Incarnate,
despise not our petitions,
but in thy mercy hear and answer them. Amen.

Doyle, accustomed to leading prayer services at his church, sent the following:

Heavenly Father, Most Powerful One, Who created the Heavens and the Earth, Who parted the Red Sea, Who caused the walls of Jericho to fall, and Who raised Lazarus from the grave, we call on You to hear our prayers and lamentations for the suffering of Rogelio. He is in mortal danger and torment and needs the assistance that only You, the one true and mighty God, can provide. We beseech Thee to drive this devil from Rogelio's body and to rid him of all disease so that he may rise from his bed and be restored to full health and vitality. We are sinners who are not worthy of Thy care, but we now come to You in the name of Your Son, Jesus Christ, whose precious death and glorious resurrection redeemed us of our sins. We put our faith and hope in Jesus Christ, and it is in His name we pray. Amen.

Despite all of these moving and heartfelt prayers, Rogelio was not improving. One of the problems with being this sick is that your other bodily functions begin to shut down. You lose weight. Normally a robust 165 pounds, Rogelio now weighed 130. Your kidneys and liver start to fail. Most worrisome for Rogelio was that his lungs were not responding. The doctors felt that they were making progress on ridding Rogelio's body of the MRSA infection, but they could not get him to breathe on his own. X-rays showed large pockets of dead tissue throughout his lungs. If he lived, these would become permanent scars. The body can only take so much. It sounded bad to me.

I began to think about how I could support Candy in her latest trial of faith. First her husband was taken, and now it looked like her son would shortly pass from this world. It was weighing on all of us, and I couldn't imagine what must have been going through Candy's mind. I was sure it was her faith that was sustaining her. I, personally, was at a dead end, mentally and emotionally. We would just have to take it day by day and let Candy know that we were with her in these hard times. I felt that thoughts and words were worthless. Our physical presence was all that we had. I would sit with her, hold her hand, put my arm around her. I had nothing else to offer.

Chapter 10
DOYLE

The house was empty that Saturday morning. School had just ended for Doyle's kids. His wife Becky had taken their daughter Lindsey shopping for summer clothes. Their son Steve was spending the weekend at a beach house in Galveston with some neighbors. Doyle was at work. His company, Hanks Systems, was launching a new software package, and, as usual, things were running behind schedule. As owner, president, and chief technical officer, he had been spending fourteen hours a day the last two weeks making sure things didn't get too far off track.

He decided to come home for lunch and found a message on the answering machine. Doyle hit the play button on the recorder. The connection wasn't good, but he could tell that it was Terri, the neighbor with whom Steve had gone to Galveston. There had been a car accident, Terri said, and some of the kids had been airlifted to the John Sealy Hospital at the University of Texas Medical Branch. "Doyle, you need to come to Galveston as soon as possible," Terri said. She didn't mention his son, but Doyle figured he was one of those who had been airlifted from the scene of the accident. He erased the message, so Becky wouldn't get it before he could get to the hospital. He didn't want her to be alarmed.

Doyle was experienced enough to know that trying to contact Terri at this point would be counterproductive. He could not influence whatever drama was being played out in Galveston and a phone call would accomplish nothing and add to the tension. It would be best to not interfere. Just let the doctors do what they had to. He carefully backed his car out of the garage and headed south.

It is about fifty miles from Houston to Galveston on Interstate 45. The southbound side of the Gulf Freeway is normally a parking lot that time of the year as Houstonians head to the beach. Doyle was lucky; it was not as congested as usual, and he made good time. He had to keep telling himself not to speed. He set the cruise control on 66 mph and fretted. Doyle was hungry and tired and worried. Thoughts that maybe his son was dead or paralyzed or had lost a limb kept running through his mind. Doyle's life philosophy has been acceptance. He had been "saved" when he was in college and had put his life in the hands of Jesus. He tried to focus on the need to accept whatever he found at the hospital. At the moment, he was not doing a good job of selling that position to himself.

In these kinds of situations, the mind of a parent travels strange paths. Doyle thought of the little girl who had recently been kidnapped in Denver. Authorities searched for weeks and could not find a trace of her. Then, about six weeks after her disappearance, a woman using one of the outdoor toilets in Rocky Mountain National Park happened to look down into the muck: there stood the little girl. The woman was, of course, startled and asked the girl what she was doing down there. The girl replied that that was where she lived. Jesus had saved that little girl, and Doyle prayed that he would save Steve, too.

When Doyle arrived at the hospital, he was in panic mode. He had come here several years ago when Lindsey had been stung by a jellyfish while swimming at the nearby beach. He knew where the entrance to the emergency room was, but he couldn't find any place to park. He was about to freak out. Finally, he parked over at the dumpy U-Totem grocery store across the street and ran back to the emergency room entrance. He could see several ambulances unloading at the receiving doors.

He immediately sought out the triage nurse. "My name is Doyle Hanks. My son Steve was airlifted to the hospital about an hour ago." Doyle tried to hide his emotions, but it was nearly impossible. "I have to see him." Doyle implored, "If he's dying, I have to see him before it's too late."

"Mr. Hanks, let me see if I can find Steve. Just give me a few minutes."

The nurse was soon back with the news. "Mr. Hanks, your son is in serious but not critical condition. He is having some MRIs done, and as soon as these are finished, you can see him. His life is not in danger at this point." About a half hour later, a nurse signaled for Doyle to come back to the emergency treatment room where Steve was being treated.

Doyle found Steve strapped to a body board, lying on an emergency room operating table. He had two IVs in his arm. Doyle couldn't see any blood or bandages. Nothing was splinted. Steve's face had some superficial scrapes on it, and there was grassy mud in his hair. He was conscious but groggy. Doyle reached out to hold his son's hand. Steve looked over, giving his father a faint smile. He squeezed Doyle's hand hard and said softly, "Dad, I'm scared."

This, coming from a 220-pound, six-foot one-inch, high school varsity football player who had never evidenced any fear, set Doyle back. Steve had had plenty of injuries over the years and had remained fearless. He played many games hurt. Now, maybe for the first time in his life, Steve had been shaken. Doyle thought to himself, "I'm scared, too." Doyle squeezed his son's hand and said, "Steve, you're going to be okay. Jesus is protecting you." He hoped it was true.

Doyle went to a little waiting room at the end of the hall and called Becky. She had no idea that while she and Lindsey had been merrily shopping, disaster had struck their family. Luckily they were home. He filled Becky in on the situation and then said, "Come to Galveston. Bring Lindsey and some clothes. I think we might be here for awhile."

The doctor was at Steve's bedside when Doyle returned. He said, "Mr. Hanks, your son has sustained no serious lacerations and, as far as we can tell at this time, he has no internal injuries. There is a slight fracture of the collarbone, which will heal on its own. The biggest injuries are going to be deep bruising, but those will also take care of themselves. Steve was lucky. Most people who come in here after being thrown out of a car are seriously injured. A lot of them never make it this far. They are dead at the scene or die on the way here. Steve will be sore for a while, but he is going to be okay."

Doyle thanked the doctor and then, still holding Steve's hand, gave a brief prayer of thanks.

Later that afternoon Doyle was able to get a better idea of what had happened in the accident. Two cars of kids were heading into town from Terri's beach house for lunch. At a stoplight, Steve had moved from the second car to the first car, a Ford Explorer. He got into the backseat and sat in the middle, leaning forward to talk to the two guys in the front. After the light turned green, the cars accelerated to about 50 mph. Steve's car was in the right lane. An old man in a beat-up Pontiac pulling a boat moved from the left lane into the right lane, not leaving enough room for the trailer to clear the Explorer. The driver of Steve's car slammed on the brakes and turned the wheel hard right.

The front of the Explorer dipped down so low that the bumper was forced into the driver's side front tire. This locked the wheel and caused the car to rock up onto its nose. After sliding on its nose briefly, it flipped onto its back. Still on the pavement, it was sliding upside down, tailgate first toward the grassy median. When the roof hit soft dirt at the edge of the road, the car flipped up into the air spinning like a carnival ride. At that point, Steve flew out of the car, butt first, through the rear right cargo window.

Both the car and Steve were now in the air. Steve came down first landing on the soft embankment of the little drainage ditch that ran through the median. The Explorer landed, upside down, two feet away, and slid in the opposite direction.

The following car immediately stopped, and the kids ran over to where the Explorer had come to rest. One boy dialed 911, while another boy, who had taken a Red Cross first aid course, checked Steve's breathing. He told the others not to move him because there might be spinal injuries. The helicopter soon arrived and took Steve, and only Steve, the few miles to the hospital. The other two boys, both wearing seatbelts, were dangling upside down in the Explorer. The driver, Terri's son, had some damage to his left hand, which had gotten caught outside of the car. Other than this injury, and being severely traumatized, they were okay.

The doctor's observation that Steve had been lucky was an

understatement. Had he been latched into the center lap belt, there is no doubt that he would have been killed from internal injuries as the car flipped and spun in the air. He landed on the soft muddy grass of the median instead of the pavement. The Explorer missed him by inches when it landed. His friend knew to check for breathing and then to make sure he wasn't moved. Doyle was convinced that Steve had indeed been protected by Jesus.

It was a life-changing experience for Doyle, but especially for Steve. He gained a deep appreciation for the fragility of life. He thought more about what he wanted to do now that his life had been spared. Steve talked to his pastor about why Jesus had left him on the Earth. Always a good student, Steve became much more serious.

Steve's rehabilitation began immediately. Because he was still fifteen years old, he was assigned to the pediatric ward. Monday morning, forty-eight hours after the accident, the rehab nurse came in to work with Steve. First thing was to get him up out of bed. She showed him how he could lie on his side and use the weight of his legs to swing up to a sitting position on the edge of the bed. She then moved him to a wheelchair and paraded him up and down the hall. He was still heavily sedated so he was not all that excited, but Doyle was overjoyed to see him out of bed.

A little later in the day, the nurse was back with a walker. This time she had Steve stand by the bed leaning his hips into the mattress for support. She wrapped a strap around his waist so that she could balance him if need be. The thought of a five-foot four-inch, 140-pound nurse supporting his hefty son seemed strange to Doyle. He watched, ready to assist if needed. The nurse told Steve to put his hands on the walker, which he did. Standing behind him with a firm grip on the strap, she said, "Stand up." It sounded like a faith healer telling a crippled man to "Stand up" at a revival meeting.

As Steve stood up, the nurse peeked around his side still clutching the strap tightly in her hands. There was Steve standing straight up holding the walker in his hands. Its legs were a good twelve inches off the ground. Doyle, Becky, and Lindsey were all laughing. It was the first funny thing in a while. The nurse had brought a pediatric walker, which was way too small for a man the size of Steve. She laughed too and went to get an adult walker.

The hospital discharged Steve on Tuesday afternoon. The family returned to Houston with a beat-up but very much alive son. The doctor's orders were to use the wheelchair for moving Steve around but to start immediately with the walker in a swimming pool. Wednesday morning Doyle took Steve to the pool at their tennis club. They walked around the pool for fifteen minutes and then it was back to bed. They did this twice a day for the first week.

Initially, Steve showed almost no signs of bruising. Then slowly deep bruises rose to the surface until his entire lower back was black and blue. Despite being in great pain, Steve weaned himself off the strong painkillers in a couple of days. He wanted to be alert when his friends dropped by during the day. The pain meds made him sleepy and groggy.

As soon as he could walk on dry land with the walker, Steve started going to physical therapy. Therapists moved his muscles, gave him massages, and attached him to a devise that provided electric stimulation. He worked diligently at his exercises because he had decided he wanted to be ready for the start of football season, which was now just two months away.

Doyle had taken charge of his son's recovery. Others would have to cover for him at the office. One day he and Steve were able to walk down to the corner of the block and back without the walker. Before long they were going around the block. When Steve could walk a mile, they started going to Memorial Park and walking the three-mile jogging trail. Around the beginning of August, Steve decided to try running a few steps. He would walk for a minute or two, and then jog fifty steps. Gradually the walking interval got shorter and the running interval got longer. Steve was able to run a mile by the time football practice started in late August.

The doctor cleared him to play, but his coach told him no contact or pads until he got his strength back. Steve immediately hit the weight room, working out twice a day. He didn't overdo it, but he pushed himself. When the coach saw that he could squat 300 pounds and press 215 pounds, he issued him pads and let him start scrimmaging. Steve missed the first four games of the season. He played a little in the fifth game and then started all the games for the rest of the season.

At the same time that Steve was going through rehab, so was Doyle. Like his son, Doyle had played tight end. He was a standout player in high school and was recruited by Texas Christian University in Ft. Worth. Doyle was not a star there, but he did letter his junior and senior years. His interest then had been more on getting a good education. Now he was carrying 270 pounds on his six-foot, three-inch frame. He didn't feel fat, but he was definitely out of shape. When Steve headed off to football practice, Doyle continued running at Memorial Park. He wanted to lose fifty pounds. Doyle entered a few winter 5Ks and 10Ks for the fun of it. He was not really into racing. By the spring, he was running three miles, three or four times a week, and his weight was down to 230 pounds.

One Saturday Doyle was running in Memorial Park when he happened to see Talbert, a good friend. Tal, as everyone calls him, is a small, wiry fellow from India. He has two or three doctorates and does research for Exxon. Steve had been a classmate of Tal's daughter in elementary school and the two families had kept in touch over the years. With a slightly puzzled look, Tal asked, "Doyle, are you a runner?"

Doyle said, "I just mess around with occasional short races. Nothing serious."

Tal told him, "You should run a marathon."

That thought had absolutely never crossed Doyle's mind. When he was playing football, players often had to run laps for punishment. If the coach thought you weren't trying hard enough or you dropped a pass, it was "Take two laps!" Doyle liked the fact that he was back into shape and the short runs he did were fun but why a marathon?

Doyle said, "Tal, I'am fifty years old. That's too old to start running marathons."

"No, no. I'm fifty-eight and still running. You can do it."

"Come on, Tal. Look at you. What do you weigh? A hundred and fifty? I am carrying fifty percent more weight then you and it's all fat. No way could I drag this big old body around 26.2 miles."

Tal disagreed. "My club takes out-of-shape couch potatoes and turns them into marathon runners. Even somebody like you could do it, Doyle."

"Thanks, Tal. You don't need to rub it in."

Doyle kept running, and Tal kept after him throughout the spring. When the Flyers marathon training program started up that summer, Doyle was in Memorial Park in his running shoes ready to go. There were also about 1,500 other people there. Doyle never realized that running marathons was such a popular activity. And Tal was right. While there were a few hard body runner types, most looked like your average man or woman on the street. In fact, Doyle was in better shape than many of them.

The Flyers were organized by running pace: Jets, Rockets, and Stars. His first year, Doyle ran with the Stars, the slowest group. Most Stars were men and women his age or women in their twenties who were trying to lose weight. He found that he could easily maintain the eleven- to twelve-minute pace that Stars ran. As the mileage ticked up, he dropped ten more pounds. He felt like he was back in college. That January he completed the Houston Marathon in a respectable five hours. That worked out to be a pace of eleven and a half minutes per mile. He was definitely hooked.

The next season Doyle moved up to the Rockets. They ran at about a ten-minute pace. He had continued to train in the off season and felt ready for the challenge. His first year, Doyle concentrated on finishing the marathon. This year he hoped to knock a minute per mile off his pace and finish in four hours and thirty minutes. The head coach for the Rockets was a young woman named Sue. She had been a competitive runner in college and was much faster than any of the other Rockets. A high school teacher like Becky, Doyle's wife, Sue liked working with the average runners. She felt she could help them learn about running and how to improve their times. Sue ran more slowly than her usual pace on the Saturday training runs with her group, and then did her own, faster, long runs on Sundays.

Even though Doyle was almost twenty years older than Sue, they hit it off. They had both been college athletes, and Sue loved to talk about sports. She knew more than most guys about players and the teams. Her father had played baseball at Rice, and her two brothers had been scholarship athletes in college. It seemed Doyle and Sue ended up running together most Saturdays. It wasn't long before they knew a lot about each other's lives. Doyle told her the story of Steve's accident and how that had gotten him into running. She told Doyle how disappointed she and her husband, Lloyd, a busy partner at Vinson & Elkins, had been when they learned they couldn't have children.

Soon Sue had invited Doyle to join the Gilford breakfast crowd. This was a group of twenty or so Flyers who got together for breakfast after the Saturday long runs. There was nothing formal about it; the Gilford Diner was a public restaurant. Most of the people who came to breakfast were longtime members of the Flyers and dedicated runners. Sue introduced Doyle around. Although the breakfast club was not a formal organization, you couldn't become part of the group if you weren't invited. A few people had tried that and had been shunned until they got the message. With Sue sitting next to him, Doyle was accepted by everyone.

One of the things that the Gilford crowd did was run out-of-town marathons. They all stayed at the same hotel and usually shared a pasta-loading dinner at a nearby Italian restaurant on the night before the race. After the marathon, they would go to a steakhouse for dinner. A steak is not the ideal post-marathon meal, but steak places usually have good baked potatoes, which provide the carbohydrates that the runners need to recharge their systems. This group also liked to drink wine. They had once considered starting a wine-tasting club but decided instead to make it a wine-drinking club.

In Doyle's third season, Sue mentioned the Chicago Marathon to him. "You need to sign up for the Chicago Marathon. A bunch of us are going this year."

"Now why would I do that? I can run around here just fine."

"You'll like Chicago. The course is flat. It's in October so the weather is usually cool on race day. Also you don't have to enter a lottery like New York or Marine Corp. All you have to do is sign up."

"But I would have to find a hotel, places to eat. It seems like a lot of trouble to me."

"We are all staying at the Hotel Monaco. Don't worry, I'll make sure you don't get lost in the big city."

Doyle had run two Houston Marathons, and the thought of going to Chicago for a race sounded good to him. "I'll have to see what Becky thinks. I don't know if she will want to take a day off from school."

Sue explained, "Most runners don't bring their spouses to out-of-town marathons. Standing on the street corner for five hours to see your wife or husband trot by in ten seconds is not all that exciting."

"I'll still check with Becky to see if she wants to go."

The Hotel Monaco was in an old, well-preserved, brick building in center city Chicago. It was a block from the Chicago River and a couple of blocks from "The Miracle Mile," as Michigan Avenue was called by Chicago boosters. The rooms were decorated in strange pastel mauves and beiges with fancy window and wall treatments. The décor clearly was designed to appeal to the female traveler. The Flyers had reserved fifteen out of the ninety-eight rooms in the hotel and had gotten a special rate. The Monaco was close to the start and finish lines, so you could walk to both if you wanted. Nick and Tony's, a nice Italian eatery, was located just around the corner, and the group's favorite steakhouse, Joe's, was a short cab ride away. It was a perfect location.

Many of the female Flyers shared rooms. Four of them would get a room with two double beds. Not everyone liked to do that, but it was a way to save money. The downside was that, after the race, you didn't have your own bathroom and bed to go back to. Sue was not worried about the money and got her own room. Doyle had also gotten his own room. The male Flyers didn't usually share rooms, but this year Myles and Pete, trying to save a few bucks, were sharing a room. Doyle had hoped that Becky would come with him, but she had tests to grade that weekend and didn't want to fly all the way across the country just to watch him run.

When they arrived in Chicago on Friday, it was quite warm. In fact, temperatures had been well above normal for the previous two weeks. Luckily, Sunday morning dawned clear and crisp. It was ideal running weather. Sue failed to run her goal time of four hours, but she had known all along that it was going to be a difficult race. She had foolishly maxed out on a half-marathon two weeks before and was still tired and sore from that run. Doyle finished in just under five hours. It was not as fast as he had hoped he would do. At least he didn't feel too beat up afterward. He went back to the Monaco, took a long shower, and hit the bed for a recovery nap.

The dinner reservation at Joe's was for 5:30, early for dinner normally, but after a marathon, runners wanted to eat and get to bed. The runners and the few spouses who came to Chicago gathered in the hotel lobby at five. Most people were going to cab it, but Doyle felt that walking would help his legs recover. Sue said she would walk with him. It was only eight blocks, less than a mile.

Joe's is a great place for a party, especially if you are female. All the waiters are good-looking young men, and they readily flirt with women of all ages and conditions. The food is also good, and the restaurant has a nice selection of wines. It seemed to Doyle that many of his compadres were hitting the vino pretty hard. He liked to have a glass of wine now and then, but he rarely got drunk. The impact of the run and the wine definitely made it a lively group.

The temperature had taken a dive during dinner, so Doyle and Sue decided to take a cab back to the hotel. They were squished into the backseat with Loretta and me. The ladies were more or less sitting on our laps. Doyle told me later that the ride reminded him of one of his first dates. He was in the seventh grade, and his church was having a Halloween party. It was a double date, and the father who was supposed to drive the two couples home arrived in a pickup truck. It was a tight squeeze into the truck's only seat. Doyle's date was sitting on his lap with her arm around his neck. She couldn't seem to get comfortable and kept squirming around. He remembered being embarrassed by the erection that grew the more she squirmed.

As soon as they got back to the hotel, everyone headed for their rooms. It had been a long tiring day, and many would be heading back to Houston early Monday morning. Sue and Doyle were the only Flyers on the seventh floor. Doyle's room was closest to the elevator. When he got there, he gave Sue the classic "runner's hug" good night and headed into his room. Sue stood there for a moment and then pushed the door open just before it latched. Doyle didn't notice at first that she had followed him into his room.

Sue said, "Do you mind if I stay here tonight?"

Doyle turned around surprised. He pointed to the bed and said, "I only have one bed."

Ignoring for the moment Doyle's feigned naiveté, Sue said, "I'm really cold. I think the wind coming home chilled me to the bone. I need some warmth."

"You are always cold, Sue. You are the only person in Houston to wear a jacket year around," Doyle replied.

"I know, I know. But I just can't seem to stop shivering." Doyle could see that she was indeed shivering.

Doyle thought for a moment and then told her to go put on her pajamas, brush her teeth, and take her makeup off. He was trying to buy some time to think. He wasn't really expecting this.

Sue said, "All right. You just warm the bed up for me."

Sue went to her room and did more or less as Doyle had instructed. She was so excited about the thought of cuddling up to his big body that she started shivering even more. She could barely control her hands enough to wipe off her makeup. Sue decided to slip on a robe and skip the pajamas. She was counting on Doyle to keep her warm. When she got back to Doyle's door, she knocked several times but no one answered. She didn't want to pound on the door and decided that Doyle was either in the bathroom or had fallen asleep. She went back to her room and called him.

When Doyle answered the phone, Sue said, "Wake up, sleepy head, and answer your door."

Doyle explained that he was not asleep. He just didn't think that this was the right thing to do. He asked her, "What about Becky, Steve, and Lindsey? What about Lloyd? I would truly love to have you in bed with me, but it just wouldn't be right. Anyway, I don't have any protection. What if you got pregnant?"

Sue was not much of a negotiator, but she was not going to take no for an answer this time. She said, "I already told you that I can't have babies, and I certainly don't expect that you have any big diseases. All I really want to do is snuggle. What's so wrong with snuggling?"

Maybe it was the word "snuggle" that broke Doyle's resolve. He asked, "Do you think we could just snuggle? Could we stop it at that?"

"I can if you can," she shot back.

"Okay, if you promise."

Sue didn't take time to respond. She had closed the deal and was out of her room and down the hall before Doyle could reconsider. He was waiting at the door.

When I next saw Sue, she was walking in Memorial Park on the Wednesday after the Chicago Marathon. She was beaming. It always surprises me how someone's feelings can be so easily read from their looks. I said, "Sue, you are absolutely radiant. No one would guess that you ran a marathon three days ago. You've made a quick recovery."

She responded, "No, my legs are still pretty dead. I'm hoping that walking a lap here will help get the lactic acid out."

I asked her, "So, why are you glowing with happiness?"

Sue said, "Lloyd and I had the best sex of our marriage last night. He was out of town for a trial Monday and didn't get home until yesterday at about eight in evening. I decided to set up a special reception for him. I bought his favorite caviar and his favorite champagne. When he got home, I was dressed in my sexiest bathing suit and had the hot tub going. We ended up in the tub, naked and tipsy. Somehow we made it to the bedroom and made love for the first time in over two months. Lloyd was really excited by the whole evening. He actually told me he loved me."

Chapter 11
CAROL

arol was named after Carl Benson, her father. Carl earned a degree in petroleum engineering from Texas A&M. Like many Aggies, he came from a small Texas town. Carl had been born and raised in Monahans in far West Texas. Monahans was surrounded by oil and gas resources, but the immediate area around the town was devoid of mineral wealth. About all that Monahans is known for is its miniature forest of Harvard oak trees. Covering forty thousand acres, it is one of the largest oak forests in the United States, even though the trees themselves are only waist high. The area is basically a desert with some expanses looking like the Sahara. The lack of rain keeps the trees from developing.

After Carl graduated from A&M, Exxon hired him into its management training program. Men in this track—and at that time there were only men—were moved around the company to get experience in all phases of Exxon's operations. His first two years with the company were spent on production facilities in Louisiana. At the end of that rotation, Carl was assigned to Exxon's Baytown Refinery, one of the largest, most sophisticated oil refineries in the world. There had been a chance that he would be sent overseas, and Carl was happy to be moving out of Louisiana and back to Texas. The Bensons wanted to start their family and hoped their children would all be native Texans.

Carl died a year after moving to Houston and two months before Carol was born. His family had a history of heart problems, and one hot afternoon at the refinery, he collapsed. He was rushed to Methodist Hospital in the Houston Medical Center, which was, even then, one of the leading cardiology facilities in the country. The doctors managed to keep him alive for a few days. Although he was heavily sedated, he managed to dictate a letter to one of the nurses. It was a letter to his unborn child. He signed it, sealed it, and gave it to Judy, his wife. He told her, "Hon, don't open this until our baby is old enough to understand what I am saying here. I need to somehow reach out into the future just in case I don't make it."

Judy commanded, "Carl, quit being so down. You are going to be just fine. This is the best hospital in the world, and Exxon has hired the best doctors in town. They aren't going to let you die." That night he had a second massive heart attack and died.

The day before she started first grade, Judy told Carol about the letter from her father. She opened it and read it aloud:

> My dear child,
> This is from your daddy who had the bad luck to die before he got to see how beautiful you are. Just because I am not there doesn't mean I don't love you. I will be watching to see all the wonderful things you will do. I know it will be hard for you and Mommy with me gone, but I am sure you will make me proud.
>
> Love,
> Daddy

Carol's mother read that letter to her every year at the start of school. It became a ritual which they reenacted even after Carol was able to read. The letter was accurate about the difficulty Carol and Judy faced. Judy never remarried. To make ends meet, she worked as a teacher's aide during the school year, and at nights and during the summer, she sold appliances at Foley's, a large department store at the nearby Sharpstown Shopping Center. When Carol was old enough to work, she took part-time jobs to help with the bills. Between them, they managed to afford a modest house in a decent neighborhood.

Children often feel the pressure that parents put on them even when it's implicit. "I was sure my daddy was watching my every move," Carol said. "An earthly father couldn't always see into your school or your house. You could hide minor transgressions and failures. I felt like I couldn't hide anything."

She knew his expectations: she was going to do wonderful things. The problem was: he could never tell her "Way to go, Carol" or "Great job, Carol." He might be able to see and hear her, but she couldn't see or hear him. Because of this, she was never sure what would be enough. Carol worked hard to make good grades and often made A's. She also thought her daddy would like her to be a Girl Scout so she signed up to be a Brownie as soon as she could. She always sold the most cookies in her troop even though the other girls' fathers helped them sell their cookies by taking the sign-up sheets to work. She earned the First Class Badge, the highest rank in Girl Scouts at that time. She took dance and marched in her school's drill team.

Carol had her heart set on going to Texas A&M, like her father. It was now admitting women, and it was a state school so the tuition would be low. Still, she would have to cover the added expense of living away from home. Her mother said they could swing it if they scrimped. When a scholarship came through that allowed Carol to go to the University of Houston almost for free, she decided to live at home and go to U of H. Carol had decided that her mom had already made enough sacrifices for her, and she was sure her daddy would understand.

Carol majored in accounting. She had in mind that counting money would be a good way to make money. Also she was a detail person who didn't mind putting in the effort to be sure she had everything just right. She hated making mistakes.

During her freshman year, she found a part-time job in the credit card department of the Texas Commerce Bank. Back then, individual local banks issued their own credit cards and administered all aspects of the cards from credit checks to billing. Before the age of computers, the processing of charges was mostly manual. Carol worked from six in the evening to midnight. At first she answered phones to approve transactions and issue authorization codes. That was fun because at least once a night she would get a call to approve a charge for a well-known politician or sports figure. She would tell her friends at school the next day that the mayor was having dinner at Kaphan's Seafood House last night.

Her managers recognized that Carol was talented and willing to work hard. They gave her more important assignments, albeit still on the night shift. When she graduated, Texas Commerce offered her a regular day job. Carol liked working for TCB but had already decided to go to law school. Being a CPA was too boring, even for her. She said she would take the job if the bank could make her hours flexible enough to accommodate her law school schedule. Her boss agreed, and Carol started law school, again at U of H. To no one's surprise, she did well in law school and easily passed the bar exam after the completion of her studies.

The management at Texas Commerce had a special assignment waiting for Carol now that her education was over. At that time, Texas law did not allow banks to have branches. You couldn't even have a drive-in window that was not physically connected to the main bank building. As a result of that law, large banks, such as Texas Commerce, had respondent banks all over Texas, which were independently owned and operated. These small banks used the bigger, correspondent banks to hold cash funds for them.

The rural banks in West Texas had a special problem. Many of their customers were wealthy oil families, and they liked to keep their funds in savings accounts at the local bank. According to banking regulations, banks had to maintain adequate cash reserves to allow the money to be withdrawn at any time without notice. These small banks needed a safe place to park the money and to earn a return that covered their interest obligations. That is where Texas Commerce came into the picture: It held the funds and paid a low interest rate to the rural bank. Texas Commerce would then invest the money in more lucrative projects in Houston. TCB wanted Carol to move to Midland to call on these local banks and their wealthy depositors. TCB didn't want any other banks, especially those in Dallas, poaching its business.

Carol loved the idea of living in Midland. It was close to her daddy's home in Monahans, and she was ready for a change of scenery. Midland was at the height of its oil boom. It was an exciting time to be there.

Carol threw herself into her job and into the Midland community. She joined the Midland Young Lawyers, a social group that met once a month for drinks and dinner. She also decided to take flying lessons. The bank told her that it would pay the cost to rent an airplane if she learned to fly.

Before long, Carol was flying all over West Texas. The mileage was just too great to get to her clients by car. Most of the time, she had to land her little Cessna 172 on a dirt landing strip or a vacant field. You can imagine that she was popular with these wealthy ranchers. They all wanted to talk to a pretty young woman flying to their ranch just to check on how things were going. Carol loved to talk about this period of her life. It was indeed romantic.

One time on final approach to see a rancher named Jake, she noticed that two police cars were parked by the ranch house. She landed and taxied over to the cars. The sheriff was there with two deputies. Carol shut the engine down and walked over to the sheriff. "What's going on?" she asked.

"Jake's in the house with three guys tied up and his shotgun at the ready. He called us and said he was about to kill three trespassers. Said we should get over here and haul off the bodies."

The men that Jake had hog-tied worked for Lone Star Pipeline and had come onto the ranch to service some gas wells. Jake caught them eating lunch over by the stock pond. His mineral lease *specifically* said that there was to be no eating on the ranch. Workers were supposed to come on the ranch, do their work, and leave. Jake thought that if he didn't enforce the lease, these guys would soon be bringing their wives and kids out for picnics on Sundays. He had had problems before with the Lone Star workers, and he was fed up with them.

"Well, I've got some papers for Jake to sign. Do you think it would be alright for me to go on in there? I don't think Jake would shoot me."

The sheriff told her, "Sure go on in. Jake's not going to shoot you or anybody else. He's just a crazy old coot. He don't feel right unless he causes a commotion now and then."

Carol called out, "Jake, I got some papers for you. Can I come in?"

"Come on in. I heard you land. Just don't get between me and these

115

SOBs as they might try something."

Carol entered the house. She saw three frightened men, with feet bound and hands tied behind their backs, lying on the living room floor. Carol gave Jake the papers. He signed the renewal on the Certificate of Deposit, which Carol had arranged for him directly with Texas Commerce. Then, Carol said to Jake, "You're one of my favorite customers. What am I going to do when you're gone?"

"I ain't going nowhere," Jake replied.

"Well, if you kill these guys, you're going to jail, Jake. Even if they violated the lease, you can't shoot them in cold blood and get away with it," Carol explained.

"Carol, could you get me a cup of coffee? I've been concentrating on these no good bastards too long, and I'm thirsty. You get one for yourself, too."

Carol did as she was asked. Over coffee, Jake explained his position, "Nobody will enforce the lease so I have to do it myself. These city boys just don't take the sanctity of a ranch seriously."

After they finished their coffee, Carol suggested that all five of them should walk outside, and he should tell the sheriff what he had just told her. Jake agreed to do that. When Jake had finished telling his side of the story, Carol asked, "Sheriff, could you take these three into custody for trespassing? After all, they had no right to be eating on Jake's property in clear violation of the terms of the lease."

"I'll take 'em into town and book 'em. Lone Star'll have them out by morning, but at least they'll get to spend the night at my hotel." He put the men in the backseat of his car and quickly departed in a cloud of dust. Carol and Jake walked back into the house to get the CD renewals. Not another word was said about Lone Star Pipeline. When they had finished talking about the weather and how the local football team was doing, Carol got into her plane and flew back to Midland.

Carol met her husband to be, Doug, through the Young Lawyers. She and Doug were both straight out of law school and had moved to Midland as soon as they took the July Bar Exam. Doug was from Dumas, a small town about three hundred miles north of Midland in the Texas Panhandle. He had gone to UT Law and been hired by the lead oil and gas law firm in Midland. The firm did plaintiff work and had collected a ton of money from the big oil companies in Houston. He was excited to get such a good job so close to his hometown.

Maybe because they were too busy with their jobs to play the dating game or maybe because they were actually simpatico, Carol and Doug fell into being a couple. They usually came to community events single and ended up sitting together. And they were attracted to each other. After three years of seeing each other, Doug said, "I've noticed that about everyone our age has already gotten married. We are now the old farts at the Young Lawyers."

Carol, agreeing with his observation, said, "Well, why don't we get married?"

Doug shot back, "Why the hell not?" With that romantic start, Carol became Mrs. Doug Farnsworth and began a marriage journey that has lasted twenty-five years so far.

Fulbright and Jaworski, a prestigious Houston law firm, had been one of those firms that Doug had made a habit of beating up on when he was in the business of suing oil companies. Its partners were definitely impressed with Doug's skills as a litigator and offered him a job at the firm's home office. At the time, Carol was pregnant and ready to move back to Houston to be closer to her mom. Texas Commerce had no problem finding a position for her there. Doug and Carol were soon off to Houston.

Carol found the house she wanted in the Tanglewood subdivision near the Galleria and Memorial Park. After awhile, Doug decided he didn't really like being a stuffed-shirt defense attorney. He joined a boutique law firm and went back to suing the oil companies. Their two boys were now into school, and they occupied all of Carol's time when she wasn't working. She volunteered at every possible opportunity at school, at church, and at scouts. Her kids were her life. She hoped her father was looking down and could see what a good mother she was. She knew that he would be proud of his grandsons.

Even with her job and her family, Carol felt like she wasn't doing enough. Many women have jobs and children. That was good, but it wasn't special. Carol had been working with the Susan G. Komen Breast

Cancer Foundation, an organization that stages the Race for the Cure each October in order to raise money for breast cancer awareness. As the volunteer treasurer for the Houston race, Carol was responsible for accounting for the incoming funds and for their disbursal. With more than a million dollars in revenue, it was a big task. Watching the runners come in year after year eventually gave Carol the idea that she needed to begin running. The next year she entered the Race for the Cure. That 5K led to a 10K, which led to a half-marathon, which led to the Flyers.

Carol was not a super-fast runner, but she was competitive. Most of the time, she ran a few feet ahead of the pack no matter how fast the pack was going. When just the two of us were running together, she made sure to beat me by about five yards. If I sped up, she sped up. If I slowed down, she slowed down. At our Saturday breakfasts, Carol started bragging that she was faster than me because she beat me every time we ran together. Frankly, she was getting under my skin so I challenged her to a grudge race at the Rodeo Run, a 10K race coming up in six weeks. It was to be a Bobby Riggs/Billy Jean King battle of the sexes. The women all thought that Carol would wax me. The guys told me I had better not lose.

When race day came, Carol showed up with a ringer. To pace her, she brought her son who was a star runner on his high school cross-country team. I had been training hard, but I wasn't counting on her bringing a pacer. I warmed up the first mile, staying well behind Carol and her son. As the course turned on to a long straight away, I ramped up my speed and blew past them. I could hear her son urging Carol to pick up the pace. I had broken her by mile two. She basically gave up. I finished in 56:35. Carol's time was well over an hour.

While the women in the club all played down the importance of this loss, and I did my best not to rub it in, the loss had a definite impact on Carol. She immediately signed up for "Boot Camp." If you think marathon runners are crazy, participants in boot camps are certifiably wacko. These programs simulate the basic training you would encounter in the Army or Marines. You show up at a park at 4:00 in the morning for two hours of hell. The camps are run by ex-military types who pretend to be drill sergeants. They drive you to do pushups, chin-ups, crunches, sprints, longer runs, telephone pole carries, dirt or mud crawls, and other fun activities. If the leader doesn't like your attitude, you hit the deck for fifty pushups or run an extra three miles after the session is over. If you don't do as you are told, you get kicked out.

After a few months of boot camp, we all began to notice that Carol was limping on our runs. She said she just had a sprain. Then she started tripping, sometimes falling down. She told us that she occasionally didn't have any feeling in her right leg. Then she started complaining of headaches. I suggested she should back off the boot camp for awhile and give her body a rest. All she wanted to talk to me about was a rematch of our race. Carol eventually went in for tests. The doctors found multiple nerve and joint problems and told her to immediately stop all strenuous exercise.

Carol had never been able to tell when enough was enough. Since her daddy wasn't there to pat her on the head, she had to keep doing more. Many of us tried to compliment her on various accomplishments, but it didn't seem to register with her. I have read articles about autistic people who, when shown pictures of various facial expressions, can't tell which ones were happy and which ones were sad. Maybe Carol was like that. She didn't seem to get any feedback from her environment.

Now she had reached the limits of her physical ability. Her body was breaking down from endless nights with limited sleep, from marathon running, from boot camp, from her job, from looking after her children, from packing her schedule with charitable, school, and extracurricular activities. It was too much, and it wasn't enough. How could she cut back?

Most of my running buddies planned to do the Chicago Marathon in 2002. It was the twenty-fifth anniversary of the race, and there was going to be special silver anniversary medals for the finishers. We all have collections of "hardware" hanging on our walls at home. The best ones might even be framed along with the finisher's certificate. Everyone expected the medal in Chicago to be one of the best, and Carol was determined to finish that race. We all tried to talk her out of it, but she wouldn't listen to us. At Lincoln Park, just six miles into the marathon, she fell down and couldn't get back up. Luckily, there was an ambulance nearby, and the paramedics immediately pulled her from the race. The rest of us kept going.

Chapter 12
PETE

Pierre de Lambert was born in Vietnam in 1952 where his father, a general in the French Army, commanded a base. In the grand colonial tradition of Great Britain and France, senior officers were allowed to bring spouses and children with them to distant shores. By planting military families on foreign soil, the government wanted to convey the idea that the French presence was to be permanent. Pierre's father was supposed to be part of the administrative apparatus of the French Empire. As it turned out, he was a soldier actively fighting a war, and Pierre and his mother were sent home to Lyon shortly after Pierre's birth.

The Japanese had occupied Southeast Asia during World War II. When Japan lost the war, the French attempted to reassert their control over what had been French Indochina. The Viet Minh, led by Ho Chi Minh, had been a key factor in the defeat of Japan, and they were not interested in merely exchanging Japanese masters for French masters. The Viet Minh had at first accepted French involvement in their country as part of the post-war transition. The French had promised to leave at some unspecified date in the future, but as the French began to settle into their traditional colonial role, the Viet Minh grew increasingly radical. Supplied by China, the Viet Minh became a potent fighting force and won a major victory over the French at the battle of Dien Bien Phu in 1954. Later that year, the country was divided into North and South Vietnam, and the French withdrew.

Pierre followed his father's footsteps into the military, where, like many institutions in France, advancement is often driven by hereditary considerations. Pierre was intrigued with airplanes and wanted to fly jets. He was eventually certified to fly the Dassault Mirage, a delta wing, single-engine fighter capable of speeds exceeding twice the speed of sound at higher altitudes. Although the French continued to intervene in their former colonies in Africa, those were largely ground battles where supersonic fighter aircraft were seldom needed. Pierre found that the life of a military pilot during peace time was not much fun.

The Centre National d'Etudes Spatiales (CNES) was established in 1961 just a few years after the National Aeronautics and Space Administration (NASA) was set up in the United States. Both CNES and NASA were civilian agencies designed to manage each country's respective space programs. Pierre was invited to join CNES, not as a potential astronaut, but as a systems engineer. He hated to leave flying behind, but the space program was expanding and offered many new challenges. So, reluctantly, Pierre decided to leave the military and focus on space. With his father's backing, Pierre was appointed special liaison to NASA on the International Space Station Program. He was stationed in Clear Lake, thirty miles southwest of downtown Houston. He was as much an ambassador as an engineer in his new assignment.

Pierre loved Houston and the United States. While many Frenchmen disdain American popular culture and materialism, Pierre found it liberating after the stuffiness of France. His good looks and French accent attracted the Texas women, and he was soon married Jo Clare, a native of Beaumont. Jo Clare owned a nail salon, and he joked that he would never have to pay for a manicure again. His bride liked to call him Pete, and soon everyone else was doing the same.

Not long after he was married, Pete had several brushes with the law in Pasadena, another small town in the NASA neighborhood. Pasadena was known for its oil refineries and chemical plants, and most of the people who lived there had blue collar jobs. While Pete never provided any details about his problems in Pasadena, there are a number of pretty wild honkytonks and topless clubs there, and, if I had to guess, I would suppose that his problems were related to those. Whatever it was, it was serious enough that it cost him his job. The French government decided that it did not want Pete representing France anymore. He quickly applied for U.S. citizenship and, because of his American wife, was easily able to get it. At that time his official name became "Peter Lambert."

With his connections and technical knowledge, he had no trouble finding another job with one of the subcontractors that did work at the Manned Spacecraft Center. Even though Pete continued to work at NASA, the Lamberts decided to move to downtown Houston. The Clear Lake area was typical Texas suburbia and consisted of ranch houses and strip shopping centers. He was still angry at the local cops and wanted to move into a more cosmopolitan area.

Pete found a small house in Montrose, the center of the gay and hippie culture in Houston. The neighborhood was enjoying a renaissance as more professional types moved there to be close to their jobs in the downtown area and to the center-city nightlife. Houses were being renovated, and those beyond repair were being torn down and replaced with upscale apartments and townhouses. A few streets were taking on a European air with sidewalk dining and jazz clubs. Pete didn't mind being a reverse commuter, driving from the center city to the suburbs, if it meant he could get away from "the rednecks in Pasadena."

When he wasn't working, Pete was working out. He liked to lift weights and run. He had managed to maintain his trim waist and now had bulked up his upper body. When a friend at his gym invited him to run a marathon, it seemed like a good idea. He signed up for the Memorial Park Flyers the next summer.

Pete was already in better shape than most of the runners in the Flyers. He ran with the Jets, the fastest group in the Flyers. With a few exceptions, the Jets were men who took their running seriously. It did not take long before the women discovered the new sexy Frenchman in the club. As was the case before, the ladies fell for the accent and the hard body. Pete didn't talk much about Jo Clare and never brought her to Flyers parties. She probably would not have fit into the group anyway. He was invited to have breakfast at the Gilford Diner and became part of the core group within a few weeks.

It was difficult to figure Pete out. He loved to talk about his days as a pilot and his service in Africa. He and Carol would swap stories about flying. She told him about the time she was flying from Midland to Ozona out over the West Texas desert and two F-15s suddenly appeared. These were the Air Force's top-of-the-line, supersonic fighter/interceptors. She was at five thousand feet and not in restricted airspace. The jets were practicing dog fights, apparently oblivious to her presence. They disappeared for a few minutes, then she saw them again, coming across the deck straight at her. She rolled over to expose her maximum profile, and at the last second, the fighters shot straight up into the sky like rockets. Pete told her, "They knew you were there. Their onboard radar would have alerted them to any plane in the area. It's common for fighter jocks to buzz civilian airplanes. We always thought it was fun to make civilians squirm." In his opinion, Carol had not been in any danger.

His stories about NASA were fewer and less compelling. I had spent some time around the Johnson Space Center, and Pete didn't have much of a feel for how it operated or what the programs were. Maybe it was because he had reached that level in the organization where you don't have to know what's going on. Maybe he was just a goof- off. It was not even clear to me what his current job entailed. It sounded to me like he was a computer systems engineer that wrote machine language code for the Space Station's onboard computers, but he was vague about the details. At times, I wondered if he even worked at NASA at all.

Pete basically seemed like a blow-hard to me, and I began to stay away from him. He, though, was solicitous of me. He would laugh heartedly at my jokes and often slowed down to run with me. At breakfast, he would sit by me, get coffee or cream if I needed it, and ask about my family. One Saturday at breakfast his leg brushed against mine. We all wear shorts to breakfast so I could feel his hairy leg rubbing against me. I moved a little and chalked it up to the fact that we were all jammed in tightly that morning. A couple of weeks later, he put his hand on my knee under the table and gave it a squeeze. His hand was there only a few seconds, but it made me uneasy. His gesture under the table had nothing to do with the discussion going on above the table. He was not making a point or congratulating me on something. He was merely feeling me up.

Things came to a head the morning he began to rub the inside of my thigh. If this had been common among runners or had occurred to me in other contexts, perhaps I would have ignored it. But no man has ever rubbed the inside of my thigh underneath the table at breakfast or any other place for that matter. I took his hand and set it back on his own leg. As I did so, he gave me a little pinch and smiled. When I got the chance, I told Pete that I didn't really like him touching me. "Maybe men do that in France, but men in the United States, unless they are gay, do not," I said. "And for that matter, even gay men don't feel up friends at the breakfast table. Finally, just for the record, I am not gay."

"Sorry if I offended you. It won't happen again," he said.

A few weeks later I was sitting across the table from Pete and Myles. Myles is a professor of economics at the University of Houston. He likes to regale us with stories of all the hot coeds that hit on him. The previous week one hottie, as he calls them, presented him with a clay sculpture for extra credit in his price theory course. It was a three dimensional model of the supply and demand curves. The Y-axis stuck straight up in the air and was shaped exactly like an erect penis, according to Myles. The girl already had an A in the course, so it wasn't clear to him why she was seeking extra credit. When Myles got to the erect penis part of his story, he flinched, sat straight up, and momentarily lost his train of thought. I didn't have to look under the table to figure out where Pete's hand was.

Pete made a big mistake hitting on Myles. Myles has a big mouth and no scruples. That morning Myles was parked next to me, and before we got to our cars, he asked me, "Guess what Pete did this morning?"

I acted nonchalant and said, "Oh, I don't know. Did he grab your dick under the table?"

Myles was shocked, "How did you know?"

"Just a lucky guess," I answered.

"Really?" Myles asked.

"No, not really. He does that to everybody. He's taken a long time to get around to you so don't think that you're special."

Myles didn't like to be low man on the totem pole, so to speak. He asked, "Did he do it to you?"

"Yes. When you got that shit-eating grin on your face, I knew what was going on downstairs."

Myles wondered, "Do you think Pete is gay?"

"Why don't you ask him? Maybe that is just the way men greet each other in France? I don't know, and I don't care as long as he leaves me alone," I said.

After that day, Pete and Myles tended to pal around a lot. They went to ball games and dinner together. When it came time to go to Chicago for the marathon that year, they decided to share a room. It is unusual for men to share rooms at marathons. The women do it all the time, but men want their own space. Furthermore, both Pete and Myles could afford their own rooms.

I cornered Myles one day after a run before the Chicago Marathon and asked him, "Why are you sharing a room with Pete in Chicago?"

"Just trying to save a buck. You know those rooms are $800 for the three nights. For $400 I can put up with him," Myles told me.

"Myles, it's really none of my business, but you are one of my best friends, and, if you are just playing around with Pete for the fun of it, you're headed for trouble. That dog's gonna bite you!"

"Don't worry. I got it under control."

Myles could hardly wait to get back to Houston to tell me what happened after the marathon in Chicago. He called to ask me to meet him for a beer at the Café Express, a restaurant on West Gray. It was nice and quiet at 4:00 in the afternoon when we arrived. Over beers and free breadsticks, Myles related the whole story. "Friday and Saturday nights everything was on the up and up. The only thing unusual was that Pete liked to walk around the room in his underwear. He said he was hot, but I thought the room was on the cool side.

"After the marathon, I took the first shower and lay down on my bed with a towel around my waist. Before I knew it, I was asleep. When I woke up, the drapes were drawn and the lights were turned off. Pete must have lit some candles because I smelled sandalwood perfume in the air. My wife always lights candles like that when she wants to set a romantic mood. I glanced at the alarm clock. It was 3:30. We had an hour and a half before we had to meet the group for dinner.

"Pete came out of the bathroom wearing a pair of tight, baby blue nylon briefs and carrying a little bottle in his hand. He said, 'It's time for a massage.' Without waiting for me to reply, he poured some oil from the bottle and warmed it in his hands. He began with my right foot and worked his way up my leg until he got to the towel around my waist. He then went over to the left foot and started again. When he was done with my legs, he massaged my shoulders and neck. Pete must have taken lessons at some time because I have had pro massages that weren't that good.

"I was half asleep again when Pete rolled me over. He went to the other side of the bed and started back at my feet. I particularly liked the massage he gave my face and neck and ears. I hadn't had that done before, and it proved to be very relaxing. Again without asking, he pulled my towel loose to expose my pelvic region. I decided to relax and go with the flow.

"He worked the top part of my quads and then my stomach muscles. He reached around my sides and massaged my hamstrings and my butt muscles. He then moved his attention to the one part of my body he had not massaged. He treated it just like any other cramp and began to knead it with his oily hands. After a few minutes of this, all the tension was released and everything was soft again.

"Pete pulled my towel out from under me and carefully wiped things up. When he was finished, he started to lie down beside me. At that instant, the alarm I had set went off. It was 4:30. We had to get up and get dressed for dinner. I was saved by the bell."

I must admit that I was surprised by Myles's story. I always thought that half of what he told me was bullshit and the other half was a lie. I asked, "What's this really all about? I don't picture you as gay. Maybe I missed something."

"I need new experiences, new adventures. Growing up I was always getting my name in the newspaper and winning awards. I got into the best schools and was hired by the best universities. I got books published. I need that rush."

"Can't you see that this is a dead end street? Anne may not think much of you being in bed with a man. If you're just jacking with Pete for a thrill, it's going to be trouble. There are other people involved. How do you think Pete feels about this? Maybe he's fallen in love with you."

Myles face grew serious. He said, "I have never told anyone this, not even Anne. Just before I resigned from UVa, I had a dream that I was in a room filled with stepladders. There were tall ones and short ones, and they extended as far as the eye could see. In my dream I would pick a ladder and climb it all the way to the top. It was easy for me to get up the ladders, but once I got to the top there was no place else to go. I would then go back down and pick another ladder. Sometimes I chose a tall ladder to climb and other times a short one. I never came to a ladder so tall that I couldn't easily get to the top. I suppose it was like the Myth of Sisyphus."

"It's like Sisyphus except he couldn't keep the ball from rolling back down the hill. You voluntarily climb down those ladders."

"I don't know how voluntary it is. All I know is that this is my life. If I can't keep this excitement going, I might as well be dead."

Chapter 13
SALLY

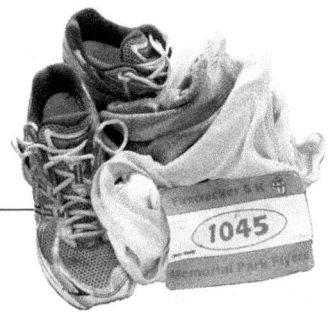

Sally Simpson was born too late for the golden days of the hippie movement in San Francisco's Haight-Ashbury, but she was determined to carry on the lifestyle and traditions of the flower children. She lived in a garage apartment behind an old house in Montrose, the neighborhood where most of the unreformed hippies in Houston could be found. She had graduated from Texas A&M with a major in computer science and was now responsible for information technology at St. John's Academy, an elite K-through-twelve private school in Houston. In spite of her technical training, her real love was the New Age lifestyle.

As a child, Sally had attended the Second Baptist Church, but she now told everyone she was a Buddhist. She had little formal training in Zen meditation techniques but had read a lot about it. She particularly liked Shunryu Suzuki's book that described the founding of the Tassajara Zen Mountain Center. Located in the mountains east of Carmel by the Sea, California, the center is primarily used as a Zen monastery but occasionally has retreats that are open to the public. It sounded like Shangri-La to her.

Sally met Russell at a retreat at Tassajara. Russell provided a lot of financial support to both the Mountain Center and the Zen Center in San Francisco. He could pretty well come and go whenever he wanted to. Russell had never been married. He had simply never met a woman who shared his outlook on life. He wanted someone who had figured out how to balance the discipline of an engineer with the happy-go-lucky attitude of the counterculture. Sally was that woman. Sally and Russell immediately recognized each other as soul mates.

Russell was one of those guys who had been at the right place at the right time. He had graduated from Stanford in 1975 and gone to work for Xerox at its Palo Alto Research Center (PARC). One focus of PARC's research was digital computing. Although scientific digital computers had been around for twenty years by that time, business and military computing was still in its infancy. PARC was trying to figure out how to get the costs down and make computing available to a much larger segment of the business community. The older computers were based on transistors. The new integrated circuits offered the possibility of much smaller and more reliable machines. They would have sufficient computing power to automatically do many of the tasks that currently required programmers and machine operators.

Russell's group was working on the low end of the spectrum. They developed a computer that was the size of a sewing machine that could do many arithmetic functions as well as provide a platform for word processing. A breakthrough was made with the development of a Graphical User Interface or GUI. This meant that the user did not have to learn an arcane programming language or job control system to accomplish sophisticated tasks. It was scalable in the sense that new functionality could be added within the GUI as necessary. It was a wonderful piece of engineering work. Eventually, Microsoft's Windows operating system made GUI ubiquitous.

Xerox, however, had no idea of what it should or could do with these new, powerful computers. The company produced and sold copiers, which were designed to be stand-alone machines that a secretary could operate. Xerox personnel did not typically work with their clients' data processing departments. Xerox wasn't even sure that there was a market for such a small computer since big IBM mainframes dominated the industry at that time. Most computer manufacturers were seeking to increase the size and speed of a central computer. Who would want such a small machine?

When Steve Jobs, Steve Wozniak, and Ronald Wayne founded Apple Computer in 1976, it was aimed at the hobbyist market: geeks who liked to build technical apparatus. Jobs, though, quickly saw the potential for a major expansion of the industry at this level. A few start-up companies were having some success with "personal" computers, and word processors were being adopted by main-line, Fortune 500 companies. The Apple II was the breakthrough product that allowed Jobs to rapidly expand his market. Russell was hired in 1979 to develop a Graphical User Interface for Apple's computers. Released in 1984, the Apple Macintosh was the first commercially available computer to have a GUI.

Russell was a multimillionaire by the end of the 1980s, and he had had enough of the daily grind. He left Apple, sold his shares, and retired to a mountaintop half way between Cupertino and San Francisco. His five-acre compound was just above Half Moon Bay and an easy drive into San Francisco or San Jose.

Russell was both a technical geek and a hippie into New Age spiritual practices. Next to his house, he built a large garage complete with a computer-driven machine shop that could fabricate parts from metal blocks and blueprints. He liked to buy Ferraris and Porsches that needed restoration and make the parts himself. He also was completely reworking a 1965 VW van.

On the other side of his house, he had carved an Indian sweat lodge into the side of the mountain. He held séances at which a dozen or so friends would sample his homegrown weed and attempt to contact the spirits.

Russell invited Sally to stop by his place after the Tassajara retreat. She absolutely loved it, even though the house was somewhat ramshackled. Russell liked to do all his own work, and while he was a skilled craftsman, it takes considerable time to do home remodeling. That meant that he had several projects in a half-finished state. The three dogs that he had adopted from the SPCA had the run of the yard and the house. He was also raising chickens and guinea hens. The rooster served as the morning alarm clock.

Russell was a collector. His office, a large room on the second floor of his house, was full of memorabilia. His prize possession was a yellow bicycle that Lance Armstrong had ridden in the 1999 Tour de France, the first year he won. Russell was not into bike riding; in fact, he was not into any exercise, but at a charity auction for the American Cancer Society, it was going for just $24,000 and he couldn't pass it up.

Russell began to find reasons to visit Houston, and he invited Sally to come out to California at his expense whenever she liked. They managed to see each other at least every other month. Sally asked Russell to come to Houston for her family's Christmas celebration. Her father, who was also an engineer, liked Russell though he found his lifestyle unusual. He chalked it up to California being "the Granola State, full of flakes, fruits, and nuts." It would be fine with him if Russell asked Sally to marry him. He was becoming increasing worried that his daughter was going to end up an old maid.

I first met Russell in Monterey. Our club had sent four teams to the Big Sur Marathon Relay. Big Sur is a beautiful stretch of Highway 1 that runs beside the Pacific Ocean just south of Monterey. The marathon is divided into five segments, and each team member runs a leg. The organizers provide buses to shuttle the runners to the transition zones. The race course ends back in Carmel. It is a challenging run with several hills, but, because the legs are only about five miles each, it is a lot of fun and the scenery along the course is spectacular. The evening after the race, we went to Russell's favorite restaurant, a steakhouse located in an old winery twelve miles up the Carmel Valley Road.

Though Russell liked to project a laid-back lifestyle, I could tell he was, at heart, a bon vivant. He ordered appetizers for the table and then asked for several bottles of a very nice Alexander Valley cabernet. My Houston friends were nervous because they saw the cost of the wine and appetizers and were afraid they were going to have to pay their share. As it turned out, Russell picked up the tab for the entire group that evening. I was certainly impressed.

Sally liked to use St. John's high-speed Internet connection to surf the net after the students had gone home for the day. She often Googled "Russell Groves" just to see what the press was reporting about him. He was wealthy enough that his comings and goings usually attracted, at least, local attention. It would be an understatement to say that she was shocked to find an article in the *San Francisco Chronicle* reporting the marriage of Russell Groves and Elaine Sorenson. The background information given made it clear that it was her Russell. Sally remembered meeting Elaine in the sweat lodge on one of her trips to California. Elaine's husband had died in an auto accident leaving her with five children under the age of eight. Sally had not picked up on Elaine being a potential rival. She was plain, even for a northern California woman, and had not gone to college.

Sally, with tears in her eyes, immediately called Russell. When he answered, she asked, "Russell, did you and Elaine really get married?"

Russell had expected that Sally would call at some point. He said, "Hold on. I was going to call you. Things have been hectic. The answer is yes, but I can explain."

Sally asked, "What is there to explain about the fact that you were dating me, sleeping with me, coming to my family's parties, and then you marry another woman?"

"You know that Elaine has those kids. She doesn't have any money, and they were about to lose their house in Pleasant Hill. I did it for the kids. They needed a father, and they needed financial support. They needed me."

"And you think I don't need you, that I don't want you? Why do you think I came out to see you? Why do you think I introduced you to my friends? Did you ever think of me?"

"This doesn't have to change that," Russell said. "Elaine doesn't want to move down here. She likes her kids' schools and thinks my place is too isolated. There's a lot of stuff to do up in Contra Costa so I go up there on the weekends to take them out to a game or to dinner. I don't love her, and she knows that. I still want to see you."

"Well, I don't want to see you. I never want to see or hear from you again. I don't date jerks, and I especially don't date married jerks. Go back to your wife and family, Russell. In fact, just go to hell!" Sally slammed the phone down. She immediately called Sharon and Carol. They came to her house that evening, and the three of them drained several bottles of wine, one of which Russell had given to her.

I personally didn't think that Russell was the marrying type. He was a pudgy guy into himself and his things. That seemed to be enough for him. If a guy can make it to fifty without getting married, he has a good chance of never getting caught. I believed Russell when he claimed that he wasn't really "married" to Elaine, but I don't understand why he just didn't set up a trust fund for the kids instead of marrying their mother. Maybe he did more on his trips north to the East Bay than entertain Elaine's children.

Once she recovered from the shock, Sally decided that she needed to reassess her life. She had drifted along focusing on day-to-day issues. She liked her job because it let her live her lifestyle, but it didn't have much value to her. She asked St. John's for a yearlong sabbatical. The school agreed to let her take the next school year off and to continue her insurance coverage if she paid for it. She had enough money saved up to make it a year and decided she owed it to herself to sort things out.

Life is unpredictable. Life is unfair. Death assures that. In June, a month after her sabbatical started, Sally was diagnosed with breast cancer. It was caught at an early stage, and there was no history of the women in her family having breast cancer. The doctors were optimistic that she could be successfully treated. They did a lumpectomy, followed by radiation therapy and then chemotherapy. In the end, Carol needed that year off to recover. In addition to anxiety about the long-term outcome, the treatments seriously depleted her body's energy. It was nearly impossible to maintain the regular daily activities of life.

Sally decided from day one that she was not going to let this disease beat her. Maybe it was her marathon experience that allowed her to will her way to health. We always say that the most important distance in a marathon is the distance between the ears: the mind must take control and make the body do its bidding. That is what Sally did. She came to our training runs with a do-rag on her hairless head. At first she would cheer us on. When she was able, she walked part of the route. She always had a smile. I never heard her complain.

In October, Russell called her. He had just found out about her cancer and expressed his concern. Sally had gotten over Russell. The cancer had made her focus completely on getting well. She was surprised to realize that she had not even thought of Russell during the last six months. Russell told her that things hadn't worked out with Elaine the way he thought they would. She wanted him to move to Pleasant Hill on the northeast side of the Bay. He was not going to leave his place.

He also found that "his children" were not like his house projects and his car projects. They demanded immediate attention. He couldn't put them on the shelf when he got tired of them. Russell and Elaine had decided to get divorced. He was going to give Elaine some money, but he really just wanted to get away from her and her kids. Russell asked if he could come to Houston for Sally's family dinner at Christmas. He realized how much he enjoyed that. Sally told him no.

Sally's response to Russell was partly based on the fact that she knew she could never trust him. He only thought of himself, and even now, he was thinking about himself, not her. It was also, however, based on the fact that there was a new man in her life. Nick, one of her fellow Flyers, had moved in with her. Nick was a nurse and had made it his business to monitor Sally's treatments and to ensure that she was properly taking care of herself. He was spending a lot of time at Sally's townhouse, and she invited him to stay in her spare bedroom. He drove her to the hospital and the store. They started going out to dinner together.

Over a bottle of wine one evening, Nick asked Sally, "Do you think that I am homosexual?"

Sally said, "No. Are you?"

"No. But when you look at me, what do you see? You know, I'm not a big guy, and I'm a nurse. Some people think male nurses must be gay."

"What brought this on? You haven't just thought of this out of the blue."

"You're right. At breakfast the other day I was sitting next to Pete. Under the table, he started rubbing my leg and then slid his hand underneath my shorts and touched my . . . you know." Nick was embarrassed to say what had happened to him.

"And what did you do, Nick?" Sally asked.

"I got up to get a cup of coffee and then sat down at the opposite end of the table. After breakfast, in the parking lot, I told Pete I was not that kind of guy, and if he ever tried that again, I was going to punch him out right there at the table."

"I think you have answered your own question," Sally said. "You are not that kind of guy." Then she went over to Nick and gave him a hug.

He gave her a little peck on the lips. Sally looked him in the eyes and then gave him a big smooch.

Sally's treatments were successful. Her cancer was in complete remission. To celebrate, the Flyers made the Komen Race for the Cure a goal race and encouraged all the members to enter it and raise funds in honor of Sally. We had over two hundred runners in the race, all wearing shirts that said, "Way to go, Sally." The $22,000 we raised made us one of the top teams in Houston.

Sally and Nick decided to continue to live in her house after she was well. Nick moved his clothes over and a few pieces of furniture. He began to sleep in the master bedroom with her. They weren't sure where they were headed. They took it day by day. Sally knew there were no certainties in life, and it was best to focus on the present. It was nice to have Nick around. She realized that she had been lonely. Her sabbatical had worked but not in the way she had expected.

Nick didn't think that he would ever get married, but he realized that he loved Sally and didn't want to lose her. Furthermore, he wasn't comfortable continuing to shack up. In fact, Sally's father had taken to calling him his "shack-in-law." When Nick asked Sally to marry him, she accepted. Nick wasn't who she had had in mind all these years. He wasn't the one she was looking for, but he was the one that she found. She loved him, and she knew that he loved her. She was sure that it was the right thing for them both.

Nick wanted to ask Sally's father for permission to marry her. Sally said that he shouldn't. "We're both middle-aged adults and don't need anyone's permission to get married," she said. "I don't want my parents running the wedding. They'll invite hundreds of their friends and blow a bunch of money on a party I don't want. I want a small informal wedding with a nontraditional ceremony."

But Nick insisted on talking to her father. "It's the right thing to do."

Sally's family had been friendly to Nick; they were the type of people who were friendly to everyone. He could sense that they would have preferred for things to have worked out with Russell. Sally's father often asked her about Russell, as if he hadn't been a world-class, low-life scoundrel. Nick thought that by asking for Sally's hand in marriage, he would be demonstrating his respect, not just for her father but for the whole family. It was to be a show of subservience. It was a mistake.

Sally's father said, "No, you do not have my permission to marry my daughter. You're a nurse, aren't you? How can you support Sally on what a nurse makes? She'll have to go on working. What can you possibly offer her? I think Sally told me you went to Texas Women's University. Aren't you queer?"

Nick was devastated. Not only did her father refuse to approve the marriage, but he insulted Nick's career and manhood. He was not a drinking man, but when he got home, Nick poured a Jack and drank it neat. Sally tried not to be an I-told-you-so. She told Nick that she loved him and he loved her, and they were going to get married. While it was unfortunate that Nick had to experience her father at his worst, they were now free to plan the wedding that they wanted. She had already found a ceremony that they could use.

Chapter 14
EPILOGUE

The wedding invitation from Sally and Nick said that there would be a Love-In at Memorial Park on April 26th. All guests were to wear spiritual clothing reminiscent of the beautiful flower children of the 1960s and 1970s. After the exchange of vows, there would be dinner and dancing. A tent would be provided to protect all from inclement weather. A card, inserted in some invitations, invited runners to meet at the Flyers usual location in Memorial Park for a three-mile run with the bride and groom at 7:00 a.m. the day of the wedding.

Sally and Nick had decided to go ahead and stage the wedding themselves. Sally's siblings were all quite supportive of their marriage. Her mother, though also not too excited about having Nick for a son-in-law, ordered her husband to attend the ceremony and not cause the family any additional embarrassment. In contrast, Nick's mom and dad loved Sally and were excited about Nick finally finding someone to marry. They were beginning to think that Nick would be single forever.

Sally had at first wanted to have just a small wedding, but as she tried to pare down the list, she just couldn't exclude people. She and Nick decided in the end to invite everyone, even Kurt, the deposed founder of the Flyers. By having it at the park, people could overflow the tent if necessary. Like all brides, Sally hoped for nice weather. April in Houston is probably the best time of the year.

Sharon and I went to the wedding together, but it wasn't a date. Sharon was still single and had not invited anyone to accompany her; my wife had to go to her firm's annual retreat. We were simply carpooling that night. We were both in the wedding party and had been given some guidelines as to what to wear. I had a tie-dyed dashiki with blue jeans and sandals. Sharon had on a long turquoise dress embroidered with flower designs. The flowers in her hair matched the colors in her dress.

In the car on the way to the park, I asked her, "How are things going between you and Skip?"

She said, "The divorce is almost final. My lawyer thought that the settlement was reasonable. The main problem is the kids. I expect Skip won't do much with them. Anyway they will soon be off to college. We aren't friends, but we aren't enemies either. I guess that is about as good as can be expected."

"Do you miss him?" I asked.

"No, not really. When we were going through counseling, I realized that we had grown apart. I was spending time on my stuff, and he was spending time on his stuff. The divorce has had little impact on our relationship, except we don't fight as much now."

"Is Skip going to be there tonight?"

"Yes. The last I heard he was planning on coming, but you never can count on Skip. Since he quit running, he feels uncomfortable around the Flyers. I guess most of the runners took my side in the divorce."

"Is he bringing Jessica?" I inquired. Jessica was the bimbo that broke the camel's back in their marriage.

Sharon laughed and said, "No. As soon as Skip hired her, she didn't want to have anything else to do with him romantically. He ended up giving her some money to go away. I don't know what she cost him. Now he has a starlet that he met on a recent project. I haven't seen her yet."

By the time we got to Memorial Park, many people had already arrived. Sharon and I had to walk a half mile to the big white tent by the golf clubhouse. It was a beautiful, cool night with a brilliant half moon lighting the park. The sides of the tent had been removed to let the breeze flow through. A dance floor was placed at one end of the tent, and a DJ was set up behind it. Most people had honored the costume request, and many people had put a lot of thought and effort into looking like a flower child.

Sally had asked Loretta to officiate at the ceremony. Loretta had grown up in the Pentecostal Church so Sally figured she would know how to do these kinds of things. But when Sally reviewed the ceremony with Loretta, it was immediately clear to Loretta that this was going to be a Wicca ceremony. Loretta told Sally that, since this was not a Christian service, she wouldn't feel comfortable leading it. Loretta said she would come, of course, but she just couldn't be part of the ceremony.

I doubt religion had much to do with Loretta's position on the ceremony, unless you count running as a religion which in the case of some of the Flyers might be appropriate. Loretta had been trying to patch things up with her husband Chuck. He didn't like to run, and he didn't like her runner friends. Loretta had been scaling back her involvement with the Flyers to please him.

When Sally asked Doyle to lead the service, he said that he would be honored to do it. He was a lay minister at his church, so he had the authority to actually consecrate a marriage. As we approached the tent, Doyle greeted us in a sackcloth robe with a simple rope around his waist. He looked like the paintings I had seen in Italy of Saint Francis of Assisi. He directed us to go to the meeting room at the far side of the clubhouse when the DJ announced that the service was about to begin. This was the same room that was used by the Flyers for the coaches training. It was where Sharon had confronted Kurt over his management of the Flyers.

I noticed Myles and Pete sitting together at a table near the dance floor. Myles's wife Anne had finally had enough of him. Bragging about screwing coeds hadn't bothered her that much because she didn't really believe him. When she heard that he was now sleeping with men, she threw him out. He tried to tell her that Pete had just given him a massage with a happy ending, but she was ready to move on. Anne told Myles she was not going to die of AIDS for a bum like him. Pete had a spare bedroom, and he offered it to Myles on a temporary basis. That was three months ago. Anne plans to take their kids back to D.C. and will probably live with her parents until she can get settled. Myles says he is staying in Houston.

Pete waved me over to their table. He shook my hand and said in what had become an increasingly phony French accent, "Bonsoir, monsieur. We have been saving a place for you. We have the best seats in the house."

I said, "Groovy, but I'm here with Sharon. We're both in the wedding party and are supposed to sit with the bride and groom."

Myles hopped on that news immediately, "So you're nailing Sharon now that Skip is out of the picture, huh? That looks like some fine stuff. I could never get past third base with her."

Luckily, the DJ announced that the service was about to begin. I said to Myles and Pete, "I got to go do my duty," and walked off.

When we were all in the conference room, Doyle stepped out and signaled the DJ. At the first notes of the "Age of Aquarius," he led the procession of men toward the stage. Behind Doyle came Nick who was also wearing a dashiki. I followed Sally's older brother at the rear of the procession. When the men were all in place, a large gong sounded three times.

As the gong died out, I could see Sue coming down the aisle in a long, wheat-colored gown that her belly was visibly stretching. She was seven months pregnant with twins. Her husband, Lloyd, was ecstatic when he got the news. Before Sue got pregnant, he was not sure that he wanted children. Maybe it was just a rationalization since it looked like he and Sue were not going to be able to conceive, but when he heard that the pregnancy test was positive and when he saw the changes taking place in her body, he was proud of what he had been able to do. And he was happy that they were having a boy and a girl. With Sue's egg problem, there was no guarantee that another baby would ever come.

Lloyd was sure that fertilization had occurred the Tuesday after Sue got back from running the Chicago Marathon. He remembered how good that night had been, the romantic setting, the caviar and champagne, the fun in the hot tub, the way Sue in her sexy bikini practically seduced him. And now they were going to have twins.

Sue was not sure which night fertilization had occurred. She had decided to cover her tracks, so no one could tell from the timing whether it happened Sunday night in Chicago with Doyle or Tuesday night in Houston with Lloyd. Maybe one baby got started Sunday and one

Tuesday. She didn't care. If they both ended up looking like Doyle, she would deal with it. The important thing was that she was going to be a mother.

Next came Sharon. She had the look of a fashion model; rich girls are like that. The hair, the makeup, the cut of the clothes, the accessories, all of them were always perfect. She had had a lot of hardship in her life. Money doesn't always keep troubles away, and money doesn't always solve problems when they come, but it does make things easier. Sharon had developed an ability to just keep moving forward no matter what. In some people, this would lead to a hardening of the heart and withdrawal. In Sharon's case, the reaction took the opposite path. She opened up to whatever life brought her with a deep spiritual acceptance.

After a slight pause, Sally entered the room. She was wearing a low-cut, white cotton dress with white flowers in her hair and carrying a small bouquet of white roses. She looked radiant. Everyone stood up and applauded as she walked toward the stage. She looked side to side acknowledging the ovation with a slightly embarrassed smile.

Once the wedding party was assembled, the gong sounded three times and Doyle, making the peace sign, said, "Peace to all of you. Sally and Nick met here in Memorial Park so it is fitting that we come together in this place to celebrate the commitment that they have made to each other. They have asked you to witness their marriage vows and to commit yourself to supporting them in thought and deed as they go forward on life's journey together. Candy will now read a passage from *The Prophet* by Khalil Gibran."

Candy came forward. She was accompanied that evening by Ken. They also had announced their engagement. When God spared her son's life, Candy decided He had also spared her life. Had Rogelio died she was not sure that she could have carried on. It would have broken her. But now her son was back in med school and once again his old jovial self. The only thing the doctor told him was that he probably wouldn't be able to run marathons like his mother did. There was too much scar tissue in his lungs. Candy read from the chapter called "Marriage."

"Love one another but make not a bond of love:
Let it rather be a moving sea between the shores of your souls.
Fill each other's cup but drink not from one cup.
Give one another of your bread but eat not from the same loaf.
Sing and dance together and be joyous, but let each one of you
*   be alone,*
Even as the strings of a lute are alone though they quiver with
*   the same music.*
And stand together, yet not too near together:
For the pillars of the temple stand apart,
And the oak tree and the cypress grow not in each other's
*   shadow."*

When Candy was finished, Doyle called on Carol to read Sonnet 116 by Shakespeare. Carol slowly made her way to the front. She had a body cast from her hips to her neck. After she had collapsed at the Chicago Marathon, the doctors told Carol that she had a choice: quit all exercise except maybe slow walking or have a rod installed in her back. They weren't sure that she would be able to run after the operation, but they were sure that, if she continued along the path she was on, she was likely to end up paralyzed. It wasn't really a choice for her. She would do anything to be able to keep running. If the operation was the only way she could do that, then that is what she would do. It would be a year before she would know for sure how successful the procedure had been. Now positioned in front of the microphone, Carol read,

"Let me not to the marriage of true minds
Admit impediments. Love is not love
Which alters when it alteration finds,
Or bends with the remover to remove:
O no! It is an ever-fixed mark
That looks on tempests and is never shaken;
Love's not Time's fool, though rosy lips and cheeks
Within his bending sickle's compass come:
Love alters not with his brief hours and weeks,

But bears it out even to the edge of doom."

After Carol had made her way back to her chair, Doyle invited the audience to stand and sing "Amazing Grace" along with Joan Baez. Although the words were printed in the program, few of the attendees needed to refer to them. I am sure that the few runners out on the trail that evening thought that there was some kind of old-fashioned revival meeting going on in the white tent by the golf clubhouse.

After the song concluded, Doyle continued, "Friends, we gather to celebrate the marriage of Sally and Nick." The gong sounded, and Doyle raised his hands and then bowed saying, "Divine One, I ask thee to bless this couple, their love, and their marriage as long as they shall live. May they each enjoy a healthy life filled with joy, love, and stability."

Doyle then asked the blessing of each of the spiritual elements, raising his hands to the sky and bowing:

> *"Blessed be by the element of air. May you be blessed with*
> *communication, intellectual growth, and wisdom.*
> *Blessed be by the element of fire. May you be blessed with*
> *harmony, vitality, creativity, and passion.*
> *Blessed be by the element of water. May you be blessed with*
> *friendship, intuition, caring, understanding, and love.*
> *Blessed be by the element of earth. May you be blessed with*
> *tenderness, happiness, compassion, and sensuality."*

After the invocation of the spirits, Doyle addressed the gathering,

"My dear friends, you all know that Sally and Nick first met just across the street at a training run for the Flyers running club." At the mention of the Flyers, a wave of applause moved through the audience with a few hoots and hollers. Doyle held up his hand to quiet the audience before continuing, "Sally and Nick have both run a marathon. In fact, they have both run several marathons. That is good training because being married is somewhat like running a marathon." This time there was laughter, and a few guys were heard shouting, "Ain't that the truth!"

Doyle continued, "We all love to run marathons, or at least many of those gathered here do. But even though we love them, marathons are difficult. They take a lot of energy and concentration. There are times when you don't know if you can continue or not. You may want to give up. You may wonder why you ever signed up in the first place. But running has taught us that if we press on and don't surrender to doubts, a great reward awaits us.

"Your marriage will not be fully consummated until the two of you, as a couple, push through some difficult patches. Remember, if it were easy, anybody could do it. The tests you will face may seem like the exception to wedded bliss, but, in fact, those are the times that will ultimately forge you into a couple and provide the bliss you seek. The runner's high comes at the end of the race, not at the start.

"You both know that the Flyers stress that the hardest distance to conquer is the distance between your ears. Marathon running involves taking control of your body and your life. It involves overcoming all obstacles to get to the finish line. For most people, training for and running a marathon is a life-changing experience as they gain a measure of control they had never before experienced.

"But as good as that feeling is when you cross the finish line, you must not forget that our ability to control events is limited. We can only do so much and then we must trust in a higher power. Jesus saved my son, and he saved Candy's son. Nothing we or the best doctors could have done would have accomplished those extraordinary feats. Sue and Lloyd were not supposed to be able to have children, but God had a surprise for Sue and Lloyd. In fact, He has two surprises for them. On the other hand, Carol has worked harder than anyone else to prepare her body for running, but now her future is out of her hands. We pray that He restores her to full health.

"And finally, I come to the two of you, Sally and Nick. I am probably not letting out any family secrets to say that your mothers and fathers doubted if either of you would ever marry. You are two wonderful loving people, but you had yet to find your mates. You came together in the Flyers but were just good friends. What brought you here tonight was the will of the Lord. His instrument was cancer. Yes, Jesus used a deadly disease to bring the two of you to this tent. It was nothing either of you did or any of us did. I stand in awe of a God that can do these miraculous things."

Doyle then asked Sally and Nick to face each other and exchange their vows of commitment and love.

Nick said, "I choose you, Sally, to be my wife, my friend, and my love."

Next it was Sally's turn, "I choose you, Nick, to be my husband, my friend, and my love."

Together Sally and Nick said,

"On this day, I affirm the relationship we have enjoyed, looking to the future to keep and strengthen it. I will be yours in plenty and in want, in sickness and in health, in failure and in triumph. Together, we will dream and live as one while respecting one another; we will stumble, but restore each other; we will share all things. I will cherish, comfort, and encourage you; be open with you; and stay with you as long as I shall live."

Sally and Nick then took their wedding rings and slipping them on the finger of the other said together, "By this ring, I bind myself to you."

The gong sounded four times, and Doyle placed his hands on their shoulders saying, "You have now affirmed the love you have for each other and vowed to keep and maintain it for all time. You are now husband and wife. You may kiss each other." Following a theatrical kiss, the DJ started "What the World Needs Now Is Love Sweet Love" and the couple danced for the first time as husband and wife to the loud applause of the crowd.

After the first dance, the buffet line was opened. Dinner was catered by Ninfa's, a popular Mexican restaurant. Just as people were quieting down with their food, a motorcycle came roaring across the grass right up to the edge of the tent. The driver gunned the engine a couple of times before shutting it off. It was Loretta and Chuck. Loretta was wearing tight black leather pants with a snug white T-shirt that had "Power to the People" across her bustline. Chuck had on a black leather jacket with blue jeans and leather boots. His jacket had a Confederate flag, the emblem of the Katy Kruisers Klub, painted on the back. He was also wearing a Confederate do-rag on his head. After Loretta and Chuck made their grand entrance, everyone went back to eating, drinking, and dancing. Loretta told me later that evening that she had started going on rides with Chuck. With her along, he tended to behave himself. He liked having his own "bitch," according to her.

Instead of the traditional wedding cake, brownies were served in honor of Alice B. Toklas, but there was no pot in them. I didn't smell any reefers all night. We were all too old and established to smoke grass in public, just a bunch of pretend hippies.

The police finally came at 11:30 to run us off. They'd given us a little leeway; our permit was only good to 11:00. I went to get the car while Sharon helped gather up the cards and gifts that had been left for the newlyweds. When I got back to the tent, the lights were off. The moon lit the last of the wedding party as we headed our separate ways.

Sharon and I were both tired, and neither of us said anything for a while. Then I remarked, "I didn't see Skip. Did I just miss him?"

"He was a no-show," Sharon responded.

"Shucks! I was looking forward to seeing that starlet of his."

Sharon sarcastically said, "Maybe Skip didn't make his reservation for her early enough."

I could tell she didn't want to talk anymore about her ex-husband so I changed the subject. "I also didn't see Kurt there."

"Did you really expect to? He hates my guts. He hates Carol's guts. I don't know why Sally even invited him."

With two strikes, I decided to give up on conversation. We were tired, and it was late. As we rode along in silence, I thought of all the changes that had occurred in the Flyers over the eight years that I had been a member. The change was not just in the club itself but in the people, too. We had all gotten older. There were divorces and deaths but also marriages, births, and miraculous cures. We were like any community in that regard, I suppose, but I had never been close enough to neighbors and colleagues to share so completely their joy and their grief.

The intimacy of the Flyers, and especially of the breakfast club, was like family or maybe even more than family. I saw the Flyers at least three days a week. We had parties together and took vacations together. We shared a passion into which we invested a tremendous amount of time and energy. Life changes: We can't stop that even if we wanted to. What would happen to our friendship when we were too old to run? Could we keep it together? Skip and Kurt were already gone. Would Carol be able to run when her cast came off? Would Sue keep running once her twins were born? Loretta seemed to have decided to spend more time riding with the Kruisers than running with the Flyers. New people were joining the Flyers. Soon they would be the leaders and coaches.

I pulled into Sharon's driveway and shut off the car. Neither of us said anything. I think we were all talked out. I opened the car door for her, and we walked to the porch. She gave me a long, soulful hug then unlocked her door. When I got back to my car, I glanced at the house. Sharon was still standing there. She gave me a little wave and closed the door.

"I'm pretty tired . . . I think I'll go home now."
—FORREST GUMP

Running

The intimacy born of long-distance running,
Difficult even for runners to understand,
Is impossible for nonrunners to appreciate

Rhythmic motion of bodies for hours
Heavy breathing, sweat, exhaustion
Day after day after day, winter and summer

Guardians of the brain's gates surrender
The unconscious opens, place and time lost
Age, gender, race, no longer relevant

Those present when serotonin
Floods the pleasure centers
Become more than just friends

www.ingramcontent.com/pod-product-compliance
Lightning Source LLC
Chambersburg PA
CBHW060121260626
47160CB00005B/1968